SIGISMUND

SIGISMUND

Also by Lars Gustafsson

The Death of a Beekeeper
(Translated by Janet K. Swaffar
and Gustram H. Weber)

The Tennis Players
(Translated by Yvonne L. Sandstroem)

Lars Gustafsson

Sigismund

From the Memories of a Baroque Polish Prince

Translated from the Swedish by John Weinstock

A New Directions Book

The present, authorized English translation of *Sigismund* has been made in consultation with Lars Gustafsson and differs at times from the original Swedish, published by P. A. Nordstedt and Söners Förlag, Stockholm, in 1976. This edition is published by arrangement with Carl Hanser Verlag, Munich.

Assistance for the translation of this volume was given by The Swedish Institute, Stockholm, whose support is gratefully acknowledged.

The epigraph, from Chapter XXII of Miguel de Cervantes' *Don Quixote de La Mancha*, is translated by Linda L. Callahan.

Manufactured in the United States of America
First published clothbound and as New Directions Paperbook 584 in 1985
Published simultaneously in Canada by George L. McLeod, Ltd., Toronto

Library of Congress Cataloging in Publication Data
Gustafsson, Lars, 1936–
  Sigismund : from the memories of a baroque Polish prince.
  (A New Directions Book)
  Translation of: Sigismund.
  I. Title.
PT9876.17.U8S513 1984   839.7'374   84-1021
ISBN 0-8112-0923-7
ISBN 0-8112-0924-5 (pbk.)

New Directions Books are published by James Laughlin
by New Directions Publishing Corporation,
80 Eighth Avenue, New York 10011

My friend Zwatt

"It's that good?" said Don Quixote.

"It's so good," answered Ginés, "that it's too bad for *Lazarillo de Tormes* and all the others of that type that have been or will be written. What I'm trying to say is that it deals with truths, truths so perfect and so delightful that there aren't lies to equal them."

"And what's the name of this book?" asked Don Quixote.

"*The Life of Ginés de Pasamonte*," answered Ginés.

"And is it finished?" asked Don Quixote.

"How can it be finished," he answered, "if my life's not finished yet? . . ."

Miguel de Cervantes, *Don Quixote de La Mancha*

Contents

I

Memoirs from Purgatory

Grouse, Flattened Against the Wall

When I was a student at Uppsala, there was a kind, genial professor who came from a family of Russian emigrés. He lived a very normal and generally respectable professor's life, with a home on Tunby Road and M.A. and Ph.D students and publications and offprints and guest lectures, and he often made interesting psychological observations about his dogs. Sometimes it led to the dogs becoming less and less like dogs and more and more like people; they learned to stop for red lights, to open doors, God only knows whether they could fry eggs or not, but he'd never noticed that.

Sometimes, late in the evening, after a successful lecture at the Society for Applied Interdisciplinary Studies, or after a boatrace at the Academic Rowing Club, he would tell a story from his childhood, which he had spent in the highest Moscow society.

From these anecdotes emerged a world so unbelievable, so absurd, and so alien that the listeners clutched their brows.

Was it really Professor W. who had experienced this?

One of his favorite stories was about a banquet at Prince Igor W.'s, scion of the earliest knights of Muscovy.

A rising murmur of voices from hundreds of guests rippled through the prince's dining room, where the walls are covered with mirrors from floor to ceiling, the candelabras sparkle, Smirnoff vodka is within reach on little tables, along with huge bowls of choice black caviar, champagne is flowing, the ladies' tiaras reflect a ruby-red light, the bald heads of the gentlemen glisten, their uniforms with guards' epaulets shimmer.

Suddenly, the double doors to the dining room open up, and the servants enter in a long row with the next course, roast grouse, which they elegantly balance on silver trays on their outstreched right arms, from which dazzlingly white napkins hang from the elbows.

On each of the huge silver trays are about thirty roast grouse, with a mild and pleasant aroma, bathed in mushroom sauce.

At just this moment something unbelievable happens.

One of the servants loses his balance, the tray of grouse is on the verge of slipping off his hand. Yet he stubbornly holds his left arm behind him, staggering back and forth with his tray like a shaky circus juggler.

The happy ripple in the dining room dies down. The officers of the guard put their monocles in their right eyes, the ladies raise their lorgnettes to their narrow white noses, their nostrils vibrate. An eerie silence permeates the room.

Alone, the servant struggles with his silver tray. It wavers first to one side and then to the other. He compensates for the wavering with short lurches in various directions.

He is now without a doubt the center of the party. For a ghastly moment it looks like he is going to land across the banquet table with all the grouse over the ladies' shiny silk dresses, but at the last moment he straightens himself up almost like a heaving sailboat.

His face is bathed in an agonized sweat; he is pale and hot at the same time.

And now the tray is really falling, now it is falling!

No. It doesn't, for at the last moment he succeeds in pressing the whole tray, grouse and all, flat against one of the mirrored walls.

Grouse and mirror image come together. Prince W.'s serf stands there with his sweaty hair hanging down over his brow and calls out with a strange, frenzied triumph in his voice:

"I've got 'em! I've got 'em!"

Prince W.'s flunky serf, that's me. It's me you're laughing at. It's me standing there, pale and sweaty at the same time, pressing a heavy silver tray with roast grouse against a mirrored wall, so that roast bird and the roast bird's image seem to coincide for a moment.

4

It's me you're laughing at, but when you're through laughing you'll send me out into the kitchen to the chef to be flogged.

What's happening now? Good God, don't tell me he's beginning again, and then with the most difficult thing of all, with paradise? Yes.

We begin again. We never give up.

And how should we describe Purgatory? That's not easy to do. If we say that Hell is the place where lies are fattest, fat as blowflies that creep over a bluish dead crow in the fall, if we say that Purgatory is a place where it is damp (against all the rules), a place where the sound of water (and the smell of wet wool) is everywhere, because the dams have burst, then Paradise quite likely has to be a place where it is dry. Dry clear air under a burning, sharp, blue sky. Strong light, sharp shadows.

All great conflicts have to be clearly formulated, all feelings great, clear, and pure, and unforgiving. Is that right? Good God, what do I know?

If there isn't a paradise it remains to be invented. Dry clear air, some trees that sway in a steady wind . . .

Paradise is a place where it is dry, where sun and sharp shadows prevail.

In any case that doesn't at all accord with the time and place for this story. BERLIN 1973. A drizzling, endless rain moves through the parks, highways, gasometers, among the cars parked on endless destroyed lots, a heavy coal smell in the air. Puffs of wind from the dead who move past in the twilight. And just like those Shakespearean kings who awaken in the middle of the night when a cold gust goes through the room, a gust of reproaches, of remorse, of remembrance, I often awaken.

And late in the evenings, from especially narrow, dark streets of a sort where the streetlamps shine with a yellow, very weak light, there also come cold gusts, troubled dead who do not want to sleep. In this city there are many dead, a rich past. They rest stratum upon stratum, one above the other, in ruins that are never excavated.

On my floor there are two cold air currents. One comes into the kitchen, suddenly, when I am sitting at the table with a blanket around my legs drinking my evening tea. For a long time I thought it came from the pantry, or from some window that was open in some inner room, but that wasn't so.

The other one is in the bedroom, it comes in the middle of the night, around two or three, and wakes me up, makes me so afraid and nervous that I have to get up and smoke a cigarette. It goes through thick brick walls, and blankets don't help, it sets the curtains in motion, turns the pages of the book lying on my comforter where I fell asleep.

The landlord explains that the house began to sway during one of the big daytime air raids in the spring of 1944; it settled, there were cracks in the cellar, even far below the cellar, and no one ever bothered about these cracks or got the idea to do anything about them. Cold air flows around in unpredictable swirls, with a steady center of unrest down in the cellar. The house has an unstable microclimate.

Berlin. February 1973. The room has four white walls, whitewashed and without wallpaper. A large, white formica table, a large bookshelf where the row of books grows like some sort of fungus, four to eight inches a week.

Outside the window is the Schöneberger Volkspark. Once again trimmed clean, spruced up and elegant after the great October hurricane, or was it in December? Some restless city gulls hover above still bare treetops.

SO SCHNEIT AUF MICH DIE TOTE ZEIT—so the deadtime snows on me

In the window a blue hyacinth. On the walls seven of my water-colors. Six depict houses and places in Berlin, the seventh Lake Åmänningen in Västmanland.

(June night: the large, pale, white expanses of water reflect the last light.)

And here, here I have a poster from the Turner exhibition in the National Gallery last fall. It's a really fine reproduction of one of his very best paintings.

SLAVERS THROWING OVERBOARD THE DEAD AND THE DYING—TYPHOON COMING ON, 1840

On the table a bowl with pens, a bowl with pipes, a jar with fine marten-hair brushes, a piece of marble from the Roman period in Salamis, a funny game with twenty-four glass balls, half red, half black (they are supposed to change places with each other), a calendar that has to be adjusted day by day and now rests at the twenty-fourth of February 1973, a manuscript where the last visible line on page 86 reads:

PLANTS, TENDED JUST AS CAREFULLY AS BABIES

I must have been here for months without having noticed it. I must have been actively occupied with something here, but God knows what, everything bears the traces of an energetic and hard-working man's workroom, everything bears the traces of life, but yet . . .

I don't know how long it's been, but I do know that I've lived without noticing it for what must be many years.

As if someone else had filled in for me, while I've been somewhere else.

During such periods I look just as if I was taking part in ordinary life. Only someone who tries talking to me notices that I don't listen. My stand-in is very illusory.

7

He can go to meetings, write clever newspaper articles about stupid opponents who get mad and in turn write clever newspaper articles about me. I think they feel really contented when their newspaper articles are ready; they hope that they will have a very deadly effect on me.

Oh yes. Just as deadly as a newspaper polemic against King Sigismund III of Poland. For during such periods I am just about as effective as the withered skeleton of King Sigismund, where it lies in its limestone sarcophagus in the cathedral under the castle of Cracow. Spiderwebs cover my face, the mummified resin penetrates deep into my arteries, my heart is an old one, thin and brittle, brown-colored leaves inside the mummy bindings. I sleep under heavy covers of limestone, on my epitaph in fine marble rests my picture with crown and scepter, and school classes walk past whispering.

No one will find me.

NO ONE WILL FIND ME

My stand-in eventually manages to accomplish quite a lot. He travels to congresses and arranges for new translations of my books, so that they come out in the most unexpected and sophisticated languages and my colleagues get sick with grief and envy at home in Sweden. He speaks on the West German radio network with an illusory, drawling, sleepy voice. He goes to the bank. He drives a sports car which he borrowed from a beautiful lady in Grunewald. He spends an entire afternoon washing brushes for a woman painter in Kreuzberg. He goes to the Zwiebelfisch at Savignyplatz and has onion soup served by the beautiful Frau Carola with the long red hair, and he annoys the theater critics. He brawls over the telephone with Stockholm, so that Stockholm gets a completely illusory impression that I still exist.

And at customs in Frankfurt am Main the border police sergeant probes my ribs with hard police fingers, trying to find

8

my terrorist revolver (police have good noses and infallibly surmise that something shady is going on every time my stand-in has to go through customs).

Oh yes, but what he doesn't suspect is that his fingers are probing ribs where no heart has been beating since the seventeenth century, that under my turtleneck sweater there are some brown, dried-out skeletal remains that rest in a grave in Cracow.

In short, I know a strange trick. I must have learned it very early, at the age of three or four. When the world becomes too tiring, too taxing, or in quite general terms too diabolical, I quite simply leave it. I live without living. I am awake without being awake. I listen without hearing.

I know a strange trick.

I WISH I HAD NEVER LEARNED IT

In old-time Russia (why do we keep talking about Russia), there was a good, superstitious fear of lunatics, a fear which is just as much love of humanity as reverence. The idiot who slobbers, who slobbers so that his whole chin becomes wet and tosses his heavy head from one side to the other; the old woman with a wild expression on her face and gray, dirty, bristly hair, who stands on a street corner and speaks wildly to herself some rigamarole that no one can understand—about them you say that we owe them reverence: for their souls are with God.

I really wonder who has charge of my soul?

Whoever, he is somewhere, he watches interestedly and waves encouragingly at my stand-in. And my stand-in, he works on, he, the poor devil, who is supposed to be in a TV discussion and pretend that he has something important to say. Herded into the floodlight at the end of a sofa! He who is just a boy, who has recently stopped playing in woodpiles and spying on girls, he has to file his income tax return and keep up with the fairly chaotic affairs of someone who may have been away for months and years and even take charge of his eccentric private life, and pretend and apologize and explain.

It should be possible to write a great exposé about it for *Expressen*'s Sunday edition, with a picture of the poor, worn-out, unpaid stand-in, who at last dares to appear and step out and sing forth, and of the cruel employer, stiff in his marble, with the Polish royal sword and orb and scepter in his hands, resting majestically and unfathomable in his sarcophagus.

SIGISMUNDUS REX

Now I have awakened at any rate. Drowsy and yawning I look up out of my catafalque, stretch myself so that the spiderwebs break apart on all sides, with a brittle sound, like when you tear silk. I wonder what day and what year it can be?

ZYGMUNT SPACIRUJE ZNOWU—Sigismund walks again

Fragments of the Inner Life of a Petit Bourgeois

It has got a little late. We have overslept, you might say.

This creates a number of problems. Like some locked-out tenant, I stand outside of my story and ask myself how in heaven's name I'll get into it.

There is only one way to begin, and that is here and now. Lost time can never be got back. At most it can be recaptured and then only in the vague way the Swedish poet Esaias Tegnér means when he says in the year 1812 (on orders of the Academy) that *within* Sweden's borders we will recapture Finland.

I met Miroslav last fall in the cellar.

There is a cellar here in Berlin, on Görresstrasse, where the Young Radical Bookstore Assistants' Group usually arranges poetry readings on Wednesday evenings. A cold and awful, unheated and uncomfortable room with a school desk elevated on a sort of platform where the reader sits balanced and in danger of falling down into the audience at any moment.

There you can meet those men of 1968 who have not become section heads in a department, government aids, or research fellows, or project heads for West Germany's education reform plan. There are friendly brown-bearded Communists in gold-rimmed glasses, girls in black leather coats with long loose hair. After the readings, which are often very poor, there is a little discussion mostly aimed at deciding whether what was read agrees with Marxism's latest experiment or not, and as a rule it doesn't agree; for if it agrees with Georg Lukács then it doesn't agree with Walter Benjamin, and if it agrees with Benjamin it doesn't agree with Theodor Adorno, and if it agrees with Adorno then it doesn't agree with Engels, and everything is abominably complicated, and if there were an intelligent alternative to Marxism it ought to be introduced tomorrow, but all alternatives are even less intelligent, and you usually go over to a rather nice little bar on Friedrich-Wilhelms-Platz called Bundeseck.

It was there I met Miroslav last fall. I discovered him as soon as I got inside the door and noted with that special feeling of uneasiness you only have in such situations that in a vexing way he looked like me.

(The other day I received a picture postcard. He writes that he is back in Sofia and that things seem to be falling into place quite nicely. It looks like he is going to get a position as editor at the Natural Science Youth Publishers. And he also got an apartment, one room and kitchenette in one of the newly developed sections of the city.)

But last fall he sat there alone in a corner and sulked, a small man in a leather coat, with a large brown beard, gold-rimmed glasses, friendly but somewhat confused eyes.

I sat down by him with a little glass of liquor and said that it was an unusually satanical smog we were having the past few days. It has to do with an arctic front. You would think that cold, clear air from Scandinavia would improve the air, but it doesn't at all. As a matter of fact, the cold arctic air at high elevation prevents the atmospheric dustbin that is Berlin from emptying itself. It is called an inversion.

That's why on such days you can't even see when the buses arrive at the bus stops, you wake up with a stuffed-up nose and strange pains in your back and all your joints. It's damn hard luck to be born right during that short historical epoch when fossil fuels are available. I don't know much about my grandchildren and great-grandchildren, but one thing I know for certain is that their bronchi will be better off than mine.

He sat there in his leather coat, with his exaggerated, large brown beard and his nearsighted eyes behind gold-rimmed glasses, and looked at me astonished, almost frightened.

"You're a meteorologist?"

That was the only thing he could come up with just then, and he sounded really frightened.

I explained to him that I wasn't a meteorologist at all but rather a poet, a Swedish poet, but that that's almost the same thing since ninety percent of Swedish poetry deals with various kinds of weather.

He explained at once that he was Miroslav Bogdanov, a Bulgarian poet-in-exile in West Berlin.

I who can be a bit abrupt at times, especially when I am not present, asked why an author from the Peoples' Republic of Bulgaria was sitting and sulking here in West Berlin instead of participating in the literary reconstruction of his native land.

That got him going.

He took a deep breath, ordered a double kirschwasser, flashed his beautiful brown eyes at me, and showed his very irregular teeth in a clenched smile:

"Everything began when I was editor of *New Poetry*.

"I wrote a positive review of Mylov. It was at the time when no one wrote a positive word about Mylov. That Mylov got his collections of poetry published at all depended on his mother's marriage to a director on the board of *New Literature*. Otherwise he would never have got a word published. And to tell the truth that would have been better.

"At that time there wasn't a person who cared about Mylov. Mylov was quite simply a nobody. Varkova wrote reviews of his poetry in *Pioneer*, where she treated him pretty much like a sickening frog." He made an indescribable gesture with his foot, almost as if he put his heel down first and turned it a half-revolution with an expression of total disgust.

"And Garoviak, Garoviak in the *Daily Gazette*—he did like this as soon as a new collection of Mylov was published—" Miroslav pressed his finger expressively against one nostril and managed a magnificent blow of the nose through the other. He missed the woman behind the bar with an inch or so to spare, and not without people noticing us at the other tables.

"At that time I supported Mylov. I alone," he beat his chest with a magnificent gesture, all conversation around became silent, half Bundeseck looked at us with increasing interest, "I alone supported a persecuted, despised—and as I see it now, despised with good reason—poet.

"Then the new guidelines came. Mylov became great, damn great. That was after the fall of the Turpists.

"What do you think he does then?"

I assured him that I had no idea what Mylov might think of doing once he had become great.

"He establishes alliances with the great ones!"

"He immediately joins forces with Varkova, that damn Lesbian witch! He persuades Garoviak to write in the *Daily Gazette* that *New Poetry* is no longer a socialist journal! And Garoviak, that damn boor, naturally goes and writes it in the *Daily Gazette*!

"Of course, this did not go on long before we had a struggle on our hands, everyone had to show their cards and say how strongly they repudiated the Zionists in *New Poetry*. All the old Turpists rushed to attack us as one man. The Neoclassicists immediately got into line. We'd just settled with them in '63. The Linguists, oh, the damn Linguists, of course they saw their opportunity, and they used it, you can be sure! Even the old Stalinists woke up and explained why I was worthless!

"As one man . . ."

I left him for a time to get a little more kirschwasser at the long dirty bar made of zinc while he continued to shout terrible invectives about totally unknown Bulgarian celebrities he neither heard from nor saw anymore. And when I came back he had just arrived at an enthusiastic description of how someone had called up someone's wife at three in the morning and called her husband "a masturbating pencil pusher" the day before the meeting of the Authors' Society.

I wasn't sure whether Miroslav thought it was a good thing or not, so I interrupted him, a little abruptly perhaps, and said:

"Thank you, I understand completely. You don't need to explain any more."

14

"Thus," Miroslav said reflectively, more to himself than to me, "Mylov never forgave me for being the only one who helped him. I alone came to his defense in 1964. He couldn't forgive me for doing him an unselfish favor."

"That's the obvious logic of the events," I said. "Since you were the only one who had been nice to him, you naturally became a symbol of everything he loathed.

"It's obvious that he had to avenge himself on you. You have to do something really shabby to him if you want to become friends again. Sell his latest worthless novel to some emigré publishing house in Paris and write a preface about how persecuted he is!"

"That would be disgraceful," Miroslav said. "Besides, he isn't persecuted. He's been on the Central Committee since March. There isn't an academy, not a committee he isn't in on."

"Write in the preface that it's typical of the situation in Sofia that such a man is persecuted!"

Then we didn't see each other until springtime. He called one afternoon and invited me over. He lived in a room in Hermsdorf, with a hotplate on a very beat-up Biedermeier chest of drawers, above a carpenter and his wife who were hard of hearing and who decorated Miroslav's room with funny souvenirs from German hiking clubs and bizarrely embroidered tablecloths; they were just hard of hearing enough so as not to be awakened by his dreadful Bulgarian parties with sheeptail soup and slivovitz and pioneer songs from 1948 when Miroslav was a little boy with a red scarf.

But now he is back in Sofia again. I never noticed that he left.

Intrigues. The whole idea of an intrigue is really a form of optimism, a pathetic attempt to bear up courageously. When you discover that everything happens the way it happens, and that everything is the way it is, though there really aren't any intrigues, then it begins to look really dismal, for then you approach reality.

That is what I have begun to do.

For a decade I worked in a medium-sized publishing house. When I think back to that period, it strikes me that I can't remember a single real intrigue, if by intrigue you mean a rational plan to get what you want or to prevent someone else from getting what he wants.

Of course, there was a nervous, half-hysterical safeguarding of territories among the divisions, the managers, the employees.

This struggle, which in principle took place in summer, fall, winter, and spring without interruption in each of the ten years I stayed with the company, never really led to any visible changes during the whole time I was there. The different parties or factions were, as a matter of fact, very equally matched, or God only knows they may have been powerless after all.

Once every three or four years an administrative expert came from the outside and suggested the appointment of some new director for the purpose of solving some previously unnoticed problem.

The new director would arrive and be introduced. After a couple of months the organization rejected him with the same obvious certainty with which a kidney patient normally rejects a kidney transplant.

The newcomer could be an extremely capable man, with recommendations from publishing houses in four countries, or be a total idiot from business school. It didn't matter, because the final result was invariably the same. He needn't have been incompetent, but he was quickly and effectively placed in a situation where he became incompetent.

The discovery of his incompetence was without exception left to the incompetent person himself, and as a rule he resigned with sincere relief.

The principle was extremely simple.

The newcomer got to look into the same files as his colleagues, acquaint himself with the same carbon copies, but when people spoke with him, *the tone was different.* That was enough. He didn't understand what he read; when he spoke at a meeting there was no one who understood what he was really talking about. When he answered a question it was other than the one that had been put to him.

Intrigues play a very insignificant role in both public and private life. They aren't necessary. Tone is enough.

I wonder whether I'm not such a newly arrived director fooled by the tone. Oh, well. One day I discovered my incompetence. The gang on the playground. The big guys who beat off in the bushes behind the soccer field.

Secret society. The mysteries of Mithras. I understand how the initiate feels when, amid strange shrill sounds from the cymbal and flute, he sinks down into the steaming animal blood and is admitted into the mystery.

The gang on the playground. Yes, the world is a playground (among other things), and one of my first experiences of the secret society within society had to have been this: sexuality as a secret society.

At a certain age in the '40s, between the woodpiles on Bomansgatan, I think I was around twelve years old, you suddenly discovered that the somewhat older boys possessed some sort of secret you yourself only suspected. Of course, you knew in principle how to screw, but at the same time you didn't know, since you hadn't had a chance to make any practical experiments. This difference made all the difference.

When you talked with the older guys about it, you thought you were talking about the same thing they were; while they, of course, understood that you, though you were talking about the same thing, weren't after all.

Throughout all levels, all grades of human intercourse in society, from the deepest intimacy to an ice hockey report, there runs a sort of ambiguity. Things means one thing, but at the same time another. Knowledge is power in the sense that someone who knows more meanings of a word, more significations of an action than is usual, has an advantage over someone else.

At last you are beginning to understand what I want to get at. Half of literature is based on this game. The novelist opens the door a crack for the giddy middle-class reader, allows him to look through the keyhole with elevated pulse and panting breath and raised eyebrows. One of the guys who had been on the inside spreads a few stories outside of school. The private sphere is transplanted for a moment into the public sphere. The mystery clears slightly. The novelist is a traitor. Just like all traitors he loses a kind of prestige, but of course he immediately gains another, the shaman's, the sorcerer's. You see, in the capacity of author-traitor you master an especially mysterious artistic skill, a magic act: making the private public and the public private.

I don't think there is a single author (I'm talking about real authors, not about dilettantish self-deluders nor about those bel canto tenors who just write to be loved) who has never felt a real disgust toward the whole profession's social function. Its perversity is related to society's own.

What I mean, in other words, is that if that is what you are after, then you have come to the wrong person. Not for a moment will I function as some sort of keyhole for you. Not for a single second will I attempt to persuade you that there is something which seems strange to you but not to me. You won't get into a single gang by reading my book. Not a drop of animal blood will be poured into your hair, not a drop, do you hear! Not a yard further into the bushes will you get. No free tickets will be handed out! Nothing will be done here before equality is established, as Pastor Ahlunder in Bromma usually says.

One of the things I am trying to get at is that there is some advantage for every secret society in being demasked, and so too for the society which is itself a system of secret societies, arranged

18

like rings inside of one another, something *flattering* because time and again it is exposed. That strengthens its identity.

To keep on exposing the truth is precisely like continuing to write against the government. It results in your allowing yourself to be ruled by the government!

Here we'll speak to one another as equals. In other words, there is not a burden, not an infamy, not a trifle, not a vulgarity that I don't consider you capable of. I don't at all intend to bring up the old, ingratiating, ridiculous authorial flattery and say: There exists, dear friends, a point where we understand each other.

THERE IS NOT A POINT WHERE WE DON'T UNDERSTAND EACH OTHER

Zygmunt is clamoring in the catafalque. I must soon devote myself to him. These last days he has been struggling more noticeably in there. "Flash Gordon grasps Diana by the hand. Ming the villain sits and looks apoplectic in his chair. We have to get out quick, Diana! The chemicals that container holds will burst on fire in a second." Won't she freeze out there, with so little clothing?

IF YOU PUT YOUR HAND HERE, YOU WILL HEAR A DISTINCT THUMPING

The other evening I was sitting with my wife in front of the TV and watching a program on the Weimar Republic. We were discussing whether Sweden didn't after all have surprising similarities with the Weimar Republic. Will we also be surprised one day when an Adolf Johansson from Mörshult collects twenty thousand supporters at a meeting in Kalmar? Will we see Adolf Johansson in a badly fitting coat accept the king's mandate to form a government in 1979?

You can certainly raise the question. We argued about it, for one, two, or three hours, and toward bedtime I heard myself say:

"You have to find ways to produce without detouring through

those who control the means of production. Only then will man be free."

Only when I had said that, did it dawn upon me that I had discovered Marx without recognizing him for a moment.

And rightly:

When I ask a question it is *my* question, even if it sounds exactly like *your* question.

Someone who doesn't understand this will never understand what it means to live.

A Breakfast with Wife and Children

I SHOULD NEVER HAVE INTRODUCED THAT UNHAPPY
METAPHOR WITH SIGISMUND; it is haunting me

Monday the week before Easter week and a mild hazy rain and
seven o'clock in the morning and hurrying with tea and the
morning newspaper and the children sing throughout breakfast,
very melodiously and in harmony: "Deutschland, Deutschland
über alles," and that makes it a little difficult for my wife and me
to talk about what we read in the newspaper. Willy Brandt is on a
state visit to Yugoslavia, and on a forest path very near here, in
Grunewald, just north of what is called Teufelsberg, a mountain
consisting of billions and billions of bricks that were carried there
at a particular point in history, namely 1945–48, a mountain of
bricks six hundred and fifty feet high, completely bare and with
some ugly iron rods that stick up here and there through last
year's dry grass, a real mountain of Purgatory, or for that matter
a mountain of Hell, bare and unsightly and surrounded by a very
scrubby woods full of old abandoned car tires, ladies' panties
from rapes never solved, a lone right glove that rests on a branch
as if it were trying to keep the branch in its place, a huge butcher's
refrigerator that was just dumped out in the scruffy forest (and I
wouldn't dare open the doors to see what is inside it), and at three
hundred feet above everything a lone falcon, hovering, on such a
forest path, just north of Teufelsberg on Sunday morning, the
police found the charred remains of a man who had burned
himself alive.

I imagine him sitting there, burnt, and at the same time try to
explain to my wife the significance of Brandt's state visit to
Yugoslavia (on the night roads between Ljubljana and Zagreb

the columns of a military maneuver, and knitted into it the long columns of trucks going to and from West Germany, and in the night funny round haystacks along the whole road, a memory from the spring of 1971), and the drizzly rain falls, and I try to explain the newspaper to my wife, and all the while the children's soft, melodious voices sing "Deutschland, Deutschland über alles."

"Deutschland, Deutschland über alles" you should not disdain, I say. It may well be that this song has been wrongly used for less than noble purposes one or two times in history, but it is really a find old democratic poem from the previous century, written, if I remember correctly, by Hoffman von Fallersleben.

First and foremost above all you mustn't make the common mistake of translating "über alles" as if it meant "over everything else." The poet does not mean that everything other than Germany is shit. He means that you should put Germany first and foremost, "before everything." At its point of time in history, right after the Napoleonic Wars, in the shadow of the Congress of Vienna, this is an entirely reasonable, almost progressive thought.

If a Tanzanian poet in the late 1950s had written a poem that began, "Tanzania, Tanzania first and foremost," it would naturally be a poem directed mainly against the British colonial interests in Africa. It would be a poem that tried to make clear that there are more important interests than immediate ones— no, damn it, I realize that I don't really believe what I'm saying; either I've shown that it's a poor poem or else that Tanzania will become an ugly, racist dictatorship with press censorship and repulsive persecution of Hindu merchants. First they'll paint anti-Hindu slogans on the Hindus' windowpanes, then they'll try to drive them out, and then, when England won't accept more of them, extermination camps will be built. Then the warmongering will come, the flower of the nation's gentle youth will have been convinced of the necessity of letting themselves be blown to pieces by machine-gun salvos during the crossing of the unjustly drawn border to Uganda. I know what'll happen.

22

HOFFMAN VON FALLERSLEBEN WAS WRONG

And still a mild, misty rain, and a Polish friend who lives at the other end of Berlin telephones to get back an offprint I had borrowed from him five months ago (it probably got lost in the last move) and reports that there is a big thunderstorm over Hermsdorf. You can never get used to a city that is so big that there can be mild drizzle at one end of it and large thunderstorms at the other, thunderstorms in the same city that can't be heard! And my wife asks:

"What do you have against Tanzania anyway?" And I answer:

"I don't have anything against Tanzania, I have nothing against Byzantium during Emperor Constantine's time, Rome during Nero's time, or Albania during the Second World War, or Västmanland during the present era. I love people, landscapes, lakes, mountain ranges, wide rivers where slow barges drift by, big cities where it drizzles at one end and there is thunder and lightning at the other. I have nothing against Tanzania: I'm just sorry about what's going to happen in Tanzania. And if it doesn't happen in Tanzania, it will certainly happen somewhere else. What I object to is not the countries and peoples. I object to what history does to them."

The children now sing in Swedish and discover that in the first line there is one syllable too few if you try to sing:

"Tyskland, Tyskland, framför allt!"

Since I am the undisputed metrical expert at this breakfast table, I am asked to find a solution. That's very easy I say. You sing "plikten" ("duty"), instead of "Tyskland," of course. Then you don't have to take a stand on a bunch of awkward questions, you get out of making yourselves guilty of supporting inflammatory campaigns against a poor, innocent Third World country in Africa like Tanzania. It's amazing how much trouble you get out of if you simply refrain from seizing upon unpleasant details and stick with something fairly abstract.

"Now let's sing together:

"Plikten, plikten framför allt!"

And we keep on singing until the children discover that that doesn't work either, and the very last chance has come for them to catch the bus which will take them a few miles or so into the city, so they can make it in time to class at the little Swedish school on Landhausstrasse.

And again the burnt man sitting on the path. Beside him was found, according to the police report, two gasoline cans and a used match.

YOU DON'T HAVE TIME TO STICK IT BACK INTO THE MATCHBOX

March was warm and clear. There were positively marvelous days in March. I remember, for example, that afternoon in the middle of the month when we were out in Grunewald and went and saw Katrin and Arwed in that nice little castle carriage house near Hundekehlensee, what fine, mild sunshine there was over the whole city. But that's another story.

A circular room with windows pointing north, south, east, and west is really the most beautiful form of room there is. The light is dispersed so evenly.

Now we've had drizzle for three weeks. Coal smoke hangs bluish over the streets at dusk. The linden trees still haven't blossomed but stand there with their heavy, sticky buds and gape. But migratory birds on their way home to Sweden are flying over the city. Early this morning I saw wild geese. I hope they don't get into the air corridors and get swallowed up by the air intake of some Boeing 727. That falcon hovers so often over the English war cemetery on Heerstrasse that I almost wonder whether it is on the lookout for something special.

Now the devil only knows what they're doing with my home province (they're letting it rust, agricultural machines stand in the

24

fields rusting, that's what they're doing with it), but in my child-hood Västmanland was still very nice.

What I remember best of all is the smell of the lakes; brown, humus-filled lakes. Lakes over which the summer wind drifts. Lakes where flocks of birds returning home scream above black pools of rippling water opened by the April wind.

There is nothing I miss here in Berlin as much as lakes like that. These dark green Prussian marl-pit lakes with their dense birch forests around the shores frighten me.

When I walk along Schlachtensee or Nicolassee, in the shadow of the tall green trees, I always think I'll be overtaken by the dogs of some feudal hunting party with their red-coated master in the lead and cut to pieces by the same strong, lively dogs to the sound of merry hunting bugles.

Prussian lakes don't smell.

The outhouse at Ramnäs combined the scent of humus-rich Västmanland lakes, where short, lively waves lap against the shore, with outhouse smell and the smell of fresh pine trees.

There were rather large spaces, quarter-inch slits between each of the wooden planks, so that the lake wind swept in. The sunshine made tiger-stripes on the opposite wall.

This outhouse was decorated in a rustic manner with clipped-out newspaper pictures, colorful old comic strips from the early '40s when the house was built.

On the sun-striped wall, some clippings of Flash Gordon. They are on some unusually dangerous planet, caught in what seems to be Emperor Ming's private laboratory. Flash Gordon, with gloves and topboots, and that girl he always has with him, dressed in a negligee which would probably be perfect in a suite at a luxury hotel in New York, but which doesn't look quite right on someone caught in a glass container (the two lovers confined in a glass bubble: Hieronymus Bosch, *The Garden of Earthly Delights*) in a laboratory on a strange planet.

The irascible Emperor Ming sits on some sort of throne, with his long black beard and his narrow (Polish aristocrat) head, observing the couple.

In the next panel (some must have got lost when the strip was pasted up at the beginning of the '40s) is the couple, the girl in the beautiful blue negligee with slits where her shapely legs are revealed, all the way up to her hips (she is really a lady), and Flash Gordon, already on his way out of the room. Some dangerous chemical liquid has flowed out onto the floor, Emperor Ming (Sigismund?) has got halfway up from his throne, he looks very pale. The floor is burning.

"Diana, get out of here fast, in a moment the whole building will be in flames!"

As a matter of fact, you can go on describing this picture forever. Do I need to point out that Emperor Ming is a father figure and that an Oedipal interpretation of the situation is, as a matter of fact, almost obvious? Do I need to point out what sort of fire this is that spreads quickly?

Do I need to point out that this fatherly evil king watching over the two lovers enclosed in the glass bubble is, actually, a very typical alchemical scene? Emperor Ming is the alchemist who has produced two homunculi, Adam and Eve, in his retort. It is an intermediate step in the process which will lead to the philosopher's stone.

And now every alchemist's nightmare occurs: they break out.

(Why doesn't a publisher publish *Mutus Liber* in a popular edition? That is the only really useful book there is if you want to understand yourself and your dreams.)

This beastly Sigismund who has been pursuing me for six weeks is more dangerous, more important than I believed!

This picture, this truly remarkable picture, whose flakes must have fallen off that windblown outhouse in wooded Västmanland dotted with lakes fifteen years ago, would never have come to me again if it hadn't been that I have once again landed in a scrape with Marxist literary criticism.

My opinion of Marxist literary criticism is that it doesn't exist.

26

What there is are schools, tendencies, heresies. There is Georg Lukács who doesn't agree with Bertolt Brecht, Brecht who doesn't agree with Franz Mehring, Mehring who doesn't agree with . . .

During the last years of my time as editor of *Bonniers Literary Magazine*, I published a great deal of Marxist literary criticism. I considered it a holy duty to give the stolid, opportune, ingratiating souls who for some decades had been falling into hysterical sobs over every new lyric poet shouting about his cosmic heartthrobs, his Solitude and his Sympathy, a shaking by publishing work that for once treated literature as if it had something to do with life, the life we live.

That led to some shabby attacks in the small town press and a couple of unusually cheap attempts to stop our publication: in short, nothing serious, but here I am still sitting, several springs later, and brooding about whether after all, perhaps, if you change a couple of premises . . .

It would be such a great relief if you could explain such mysterious things as works of art, in a fully natural, healthy, rational way, as the final outcome of a period's order of production.

I've been struggling with the problem for years, and now and then I get a new idea.

Right now it's Walter Benjamin. The question is whether he is a Marxist literary critic or not. He is a little *too* responsive to what remains in a work of art after the rough materialistic sieve has taken its share, a little *too* dialectic, a little *too* heretical. That is what entices me.

Thus:

Since the children had taken their bus to school and my wife had sat down at the kitchen table with her drama translation and her ridiculous jar of candy and her sketches, I sank into Benjamin. The so-called Passagework never finished because the Nazis didn't give him a chance, a brilliant attempt to let the entire preceding

27

century unfold before your eyes with the help of Baudelaire's poetry, certain labyrinthine features in the public image of Paris in the 1880s and the droves of people on the sidewalks, the experience of the big city.

Now it turns out there are in fact two versions of Benjamin's Passagework.

It is a rather amusing story. You could write a decent novel about it.

Later in the afternoon, therefore, I paid a visit to my friend Zwatt to have myself instructed about the different versions by an intelligent person who really knows something about the matter.

I swear by everything that is holy to me that I did nothing more remarkable there than sit in a nice gray easy chair and let myself be instructed for several hours about the versions of Passagework. I drank a couple pots of tea as well, but that has little to do with it.

It is remarkable that when certain people get together they have the strangest effects on one another without so much as a shadow of it showing on the surface of the conversation. That is precisely like when a dog owner in the country visits another dog owner and sits and talks with him.

Meanwhile, the dogs lie tied up out in the kitchen, each firmly moored to its own leg of the table and howl and whimper and growl at one another.

While Zwatt and I were sitting and talking in her beautiful library about the versions of Benjamin's texts, our subconsciouses were lying out in the kitchen and howling.

The result was that when I come out into the spring evening, it is already getting dark down at the little market at the Schöneberg S-Bahn station. I come out into the darkening, drizzling, coal-smelling spring evening, and it's not Benjamin at all I am concerned with anymore but that silly old comic strip with the lovers caught in the glass container and watched over by that frightful old man with the black, forked beard and the corners of his mouth pulled down fiercely. With strange power it shines at me through the drizzle, and I haven't thought about this picture, I swear, in twenty years, and I didn't talk about it during my visit, and now it is as if the entire visit was aimed at bringing that picture back to life for me again. It has been lying very still in some dark corner behind my eyes. The social-democratic postwar program, the Korean War, the long decade of the '60s, the nuclear threat, and the Vietnam War have passed by without this picture having moved an inch from its place behind my eyes.

But now, in a friendly library, in a gray easy chair, with drizzle like wet gloves against the windowpanes and the diffuse coronas of the gaslights outside, with the clatter of teacups and a quiet, unobtrusive conversation about things that lie far away,

NOW IT MOVED

An Intergalactic War

For a couple of decades, Fleet 15 has been patrolling space A2811—B16791—C632, in other words, very close to the outermost spiral arms of the Milky Way. That it is a reconnaissance fleet with the task of mapping suitable positions for attack has been known for millennia.

Presumably for just as many millennia it has been marked as a red dot, or perhaps a red triangle, on various plotting boards in deep subterranean rooms on apparently lifeless and nitric acid-smelling giant planets in dead sun systems on the periphery of the home galaxy.

In other strategic command centers on more populous and, above all, better defended planets around the old central suns at the center of the galaxy, it was also noted on the large glass tanks of the situation maps. The triangle moved slowly, infinitely more slowly than the hands on a clock, month after month, year after year, along its hyperbolic orbit on the maps.

With this difference: that on the large glass tanks of the situation maps you could see other such triangles, at entirely opposite ends of the galaxy. They moved at the same slow pace, they've also been there for roughly twenty thousand years.

What was not shown on the situation maps of the outermost patrol and early-warning stations, but surely on those around the central sun, were the invisible powers (blue circles) that were watching the intruders.

Unfalteringly the blue circles followed the red triangles decade after decade on their swift journey through the darkness of the outermost spiral arms, through intergalactic dustclouds that prevented radio communication for months and years, in and out through the spiral arms' bays, capes, and strange tunnels of starless, desolate space. Invisible, without radio contact, bodyless, units of the Special Reconnaissance Corps have been sending, decade after decade, a never-ceasing stream of telemetrics, co-

30

ordinates, detailed diagrams, pictures, biological analyses of the intruders directly to the central strategic command centers.

There was no doubt that the intruders came from Andromeda. This was no accidental band of marauders, no civilization on the march after some ruined, primitive, peripheral civilization had been blown away by some supernova. It was really the central civilization in the distant galaxy's enigmatic, inner realms that, for some incomprehensible reason, sounded and measured the reaches of space beyond the home galaxy's outermost spiral arms.

The central administration's essential attitude was of chilly curiosity, mixed with careful expectations. On this plane, where we now find ourselves, fear does not exist, since there is basically nothing to fear. But curiosity exists, and so do love and hate.

In the presence of something *really alien*, love and hate are almost impossible to distinguish from each other.

Intergalactic war is aimed not so much at destruction—how could you destroy a galaxy—nor at wiping out life—wiping out life on the cosmic scale infallibly leads to another life arising somewhere else which purposefully develops, even if it takes billions of years, up to the point where it is especially equipped for wiping out your own. Galactic civilizations have made enough mistakes through the ages to have learned that lesson.

Intergalactic wars are not simply wars, they are just as much something sexual, great fertilizations where mature, rich, top-heavy civilizations take the leap over millions of light-years and touch each other. It is serious enough. Where can such an act of fertilization lead: nothing being as before.

On the galactic plane change, not death, is the great problem; the new birth, not orgasm, is what is worth striving for.

What is now happening, and what has been going on for epochs, can best be likened to what happens when two dachshunds meet on a sidewalk and with extreme caution begin to sniff each other.

An eccentric nature has constructed us so that we dislike living in concentrated sulfuric acid at an atmospheric pressure of 200 kilograms per square centimeter and a temperature 183 degrees Celsius.

It's too bad, for in the plotting room on the planet Melahim, near one of the Milky Way's ancient suns a good bit above our own in mass and spectral class even though it is significantly older, in the plotting room, two thousand feet below land surface in the subterranean city of Of, below the quiet countryside on the legendary continent Agfa, a masterly simple, maintenance-free control device without movable parts keeps the sulfuric acid at exactly two hundred atmospheres and 183 degrees.

You see, it is a tried and proved fact that the personnel at this center, who work in shifts of one hundred and sixty-three days and then devote themselves to pleasures (some of which are sophisticated) and sleep for several hundred days, actually thrive and work best at 183 degrees.

Life on Melahim, as on all planets up to several light-years away, is, actually, somewhat conservatively organized on the basis of a sulfur-hydrogen cycle and rather substantial mass relationships, quite unlike our adventurous fluttering about like butterflies in an oxygen-carbon dioxide cycle under pressure relationships bordering on vacuum and temperature relationships that would cause an inhabitant of Melahim to be transformed into a fragile piece of crystal in less than a second.

(For that matter, I can mention that my grandfather's watch, which is lying so nicely and ticking on my writing table, actually would weight two hundred and eight kilos on Melahim.)

So, we have to imagine that we are floating around in sulfuric acid (like a bluish, stylized jellyfish about forty feet in diameter at its thickest, thousands of cilia hanging down from the jellyfish bell, some of us indolent and absent-mindedly whisking in the sulfuric acid, others active, searching, conversing, fingering the control board's hundreds of light points) up to one of the central control boards and fondle some switches that couple us in to Blue Unity Ygris 15, which has been keeping an eye on Andromeda's Fleet 15 since October (that both are numbered 15 is no accident).

It takes a little while for the signals to arrive. If they were the usual ordinary radio waves we would have to sit and wait for three and a half years, but now the screen is actually beginning to light up.

There we have the huge shadow of the admiral ship of Fleet 15, as large as the earth's circumference at the equator, but without a single opening. It looks like a rather ordinary flattened plum floating through space, with the flat ends up and down.

Let's see now, now we'll turn the wheel just slightly—it has a scorpion-shaped insignia, no, we won't turn the wheel, we'll move just one cilium in a gentle movement around it, on the whole there don't seem to be any moving parts here, let's see if we can get some good interior pictures.

What the hell is this thing here? It looks like a narrow rod or a pipe, with some small colored sparkling bodies or dots in a channel inside the rod. (Excellent color reception by the way, but how do you know they are the right colors?) There is constant movement and sparkling inside the pipe, but what in hell is moving and sparkling?

Now I know. It's *a virus*! Or is it? It might be forty feet long. What are we measuring by?

"Yes, Sir," says Sergeant Is-Izt, who is just peering over our shoulders and watching the screen, "what sort of thing it really is isn't easy to say. Andromeda is a distant galaxy, it's really a very alien life, you can't expect our apparatus to be able to capture it *visually*, if that's what Dr. Gustafsson is expecting, excuse me, Mr. Gustafsson, Sir. What we see here is quite certainly a virus. Viruses in our galaxy are a basic form of life, you understand; what the apparatus is showing on the screen is not so much a picture as a symbol, a graphic sign, if you want, Sir.

"We may not infer that the craft is populated by viruses, but only that whatever it is that the apparatus picks up, it more nearly reminds it of a virus than anything else. All knowledge demands that you compare something that you don't know with something you know, isn't that right, Sir?

"What is really inside that dark craft we don't know. It is life. It is an admiral ship in a reconnaissance fleet from the central civilization in the Andromeda galaxy. It is systematically searching out areas of deployment for an attack.

"We have no idea what it is really up to."

"What does it look like between the viruses? What is the *arrangement* like?"

"Quite compact. As compact as basalt rock."

The sergeant obligingly caresses his wheel again.

What appears looks like an X-ray crystallogram. More or less diffuse circles at exactly the same distance from each other.

"Viruses frozen in basalt rock?"

"Yes," answers the sergeant, and laughs an unimaginably ironic laugh with some pale blue threads of cilia in a small, determined undulation. It looks as though our friends are in no great hurry.

"It takes pretty tough stuff to travel through intergalactic space. There are gravitation waves that'll blow away a couple of desolate suns about as easily as you blow away pipe smoke, and huge dark clouds of dust containing who the hell knows what.

"I think, with your permission, Sir, that the admiral ship is about as sensibly constructed as an admiral ship of that sort ought to be. But would you care for a cup of tea? We always drink a little tea about this time in the afternoon to keep our thoughts clear.

"Are you done looking, Sir? As you see from the crystal structure it is a single, compact, extremely hard mountain of rock, a tower of basalt if you please, and something inside that mountain is thinking and living and wants something. Sugar, Sir? How many lumps? I see, three."

He whisked over the control panel, and the image disappeared, replaced by a reddish-purple monotone surface.

"Sir, you understand, the interesting thing about Fleet 15 is not how it looks. What bewilders us is how it behaves. It is signaling back to Andromeda. Wait, you'll see."

Some more whiskings at the control panel caused not only one, but two, three, four screens to light up. On the one furthest to the left was something that looked like an insanely complicated cathode-ray oscillogram, with such a high frequency and so dense that it filled the whole screen with its swiftly moving, white lines. It bore a certain similarity to the voice of a mad amateur opera singer.

"Yes," said Sergeant Is-Izt, "that is a very dense signal you see. We have calculated that it has an information density of about 148K bits per second. It would be able to handle the University Library in Uppsala in a couple of hours. The signal is a superpulse laid on top of a gamma wave, it goes about ten thousand times quicker than the speed of light. Of course, the signal doesn't exist in any physical sense, in which case it wouldn't be able to go faster than the speed of light. It exists in the same way as the sense of a poem by Gunnar Ekelöf exists, regardless of whether you print it in Gothic script or not.

"For intergalactic conditions it is a rather common arrangement. It took us just a couple hundred years to decipher it. We have most of it recorded.

"On the first kilometers of the band it handles quite obvious things. Telemetrics, endless quantities of telemetrics. The closer it gets to the outer spiral arms of our galaxy the more it becomes interested in the masses and spectral classes of the various stars. It measures them, verifies the spectrum, accounts for what elements are found in the suns. The reconnaissance fleet moves in a way that seems reasonable if you want to know such things.

"But then something very odd happens.

"That is what we have begun to ponder."

"And what is it that's odd?"

"We've begun to suspect that it has a spy in one of the outer portions of the home galaxy."

"A spy?"

"Yes, a spy. You see, it has begun to exchange signals with a point in a field; nothing serious, but it is a field rather far out. We didn't understand a thing at first, we couldn't comprehend what sort of signal source there could be out there in the half-darkness, but now we've figured it out.

"Look at this diagram. It is Fleet 15's course up to—what is that in your time, Sir? it must be 1632, yes, 1632.

"After 1632, it settles into a strange elliptical orbit out there— you see, Sir, it almost looks as if it were *paralyzed*—and at that time it begins to take up a new signal. It looks like this.

"If you look at the fourth screen to the right. Could we please have it enlarged a little, Lance Corporal Ygel-Agel? Thank you very much! That was so kind of you, Lance Corporal! Oh, the pleasure is mine! Oh no, not at all!" I thought the mens' exchange of compliments and almost coquettish enthusiasm in keeping it going would continue for half an hour, but it gradually ebbed. "On the contrary, it is a very special pleasure for me to ask *you*, Lance Corporal Ygel-Agel, for a small service! Don't mention it! Oh, I beg you! Oh now, you are overdoing it!"

In any case, we finally got the picture enlarged. It was a much simpler signal, thinner, lower in frequency. It looked as if someone was humming a children's verse, a very sad, old-fashioned children's verse, again and again.

"Of course, we've discussed the possibility that it could be some sort of beacon, an automaton someone had placed there to give them position information, but what the hell are they going to do with it?"

He turned up the sound. It really seemed like a weak humming, like when a very old man sinks back into childhood and hums a little lullaby to himself. It was impossible to discern any words, it was quite simply a humming.

"That's how it sounds. It repeats at a frequency of 2.567 minutes since 1632 in your time."

"Remarkable!"

"Certainly. But what is really remarkable is the effect it has on Reconnaissance Fleet 15 from Andromeda."

"What do you mean?"

"It paralyzes it. It makes it frantic. Look at this large situation

36

map. Could we have Fleet 15's course from the twelfth century put in? Thank you. Oh, I beg you (etc.). You see, Sir. Up to 1632 it moves normally, that is, it executes a normal course for an intergalactic undertaking. In 1632 it lies in a column. And what course does the map describe since then?"

"I think it looks like a figure eight with a piece missing."

"That's right, an eight, it goes around in a propeller-wound eight, but with the exception that it avoids one point the whole time. It is the point where this signal begins in 1632. That is the little vexing notch in the eight."

"So something has got stuck?"

"Got stuck? That I can assure you. That fleet is mad! It is paralyzed! Stark raving mad! And this is what makes us uneasy. Do you know what that signal consists of?"

"No."

"Since 1632, of sheer madness!"

"Really?"

"Sheer, pure mania!"

"Are you sure of that? Can't it be a code?"

"Code? You surprise me, my dear friend! I'll take out a couple pieces from this morning's recording so you can hear for yourself. What do you say about this?"

IMPROVEMENT MIDFIELD IS NECESSARY

"That isn't so odd."

"No?"

"Not at all. They've got into a quarrel with headquarters in Andromeda about some detail in the deployment plan. Of course! A discussion is going on, somewhat lengthy perhaps. May I hear it one more time? I'll certainly be able to help you."

I saw that the sergeant's patience was struggling with his innate and, by our standards, enormous civility. He became a little pale in his upper body, but he granted my request nevertheless.

"Nothing could be more important to us that your amiable help, my dear friend!"

37

IMPROVEMENT MIDFIELD IS NECESSARY EVEN WITH
AN INGVARFLINK IN NORMAL PLAYING FORM SAAB
SHOULD BUILD UP THE GAMMON MIDFIELD FROM
NOW ON

"Thanks, that's enough," I said.
"Or what do you say about this—"

BUT WHAT THE STANDARD THAT HAS MADE ME
    SPEAK
ACHIEVED BEFORE, AND AFTER SHOULD ACHIEVE
THROUGHOUT THE MORTAL REALM THAT LIES
    BENEATH IT,
BECOMETH IN APPEARANCE MEAN AND DIM,
IF IN THE HAND OF THE THIRD CAESAR SEEN

"It's channel 2348 at 6:04 this morning, your time. The rest has sounded about the same since 2:00 P.M. And what does 'up the gammon' mean? 'Up the gammon'! That's nonsense."

"A bit eccentric, isn't that so," added the lance corporal, who had come floating up.

"Sheer madness!"

"So you think this strange lullaby has made them mad, holds them in a sort of paralytic control."

"That's right."

"But that means . . ."

"That's right."

"That's dangerous!"

"Very dangerous, but it means exactly what you think. *Someone else*, some malevolent force in our own galaxy has taken command of the fleet from Andromeda, of *all fleets*, and is keeping them under his hypnotic control for his own purpose. The central administration is a bit bewildered. It has asked for a brief report.

"That doesn't often happen, I imagine?"

The sergeant nods patiently.

38

"No, my dear friend. It doesn't happen often."

"But where is that strange signal coming from?"

"We've devoted a great deal of attention to that problem. Sir, if you look at the situation map here, the lance corporal will enlarge that field, thanks, more please, thank you, maximum enlargement, Oh, I beg you (etc.), you will see perhaps here, no not here, six light-years further away, there, at the tip of that lead pencil, *there* yes. It's a very normal sun, normal mass, normal spectral class. The planets aren't visible without the microscope, and Under Sergeant Ibn-If is just now using it on the other side of the map, but in any case there are a couple of planets. The whole thing is a very new development, but the third planet from the sun has produced some sort of very temporary life based on the oxygen-carbon dioxide cycle. Very, very delicate. Nothing developable. Just surface movements. There's some sort of primate there, striking molars, sexual reproduction on the principle of external sex organs in half the population and internal in the other half, movable hip joints, light signals perceived within a limited spectrum, presumably there are other sense organs, very weak psi waves, mostly in older specimens. They will meet with the usual fate in a couple thousand years."

"Oh. What is the usual fate?"

"Self-poisoning, of course. Poisoning of the planet's own atmosphere through excessive biological activity," he didn't once raise his head from the map, "pollution, suffocation, radioactive poisoning.

"In any case, these primates have some kind of primative civilization. The aim is mostly to obliterate one another, naturally. They don't even eat up the dead specimens. Obvious faulty development, been hopeless for a million years of course. Just shit. But in any case, there are some signs of civilization, a little more densely concentrated on certain continents. The continents move on a layer of volcanic magma and are surrounded by a thin layer of hydrogen dioxide, which plays a role in their biological synthesis.

"At any rate, there is an object on one of the continents that is

39

sending out signals, it has determined without a doubt the details of our signal reconnaissance."

"What kind of an object is it?"

"It seems to be an ark of limestone, about thirteen feet long and three feet wide. It's decorated on the top with a reproduction of a masculine primate with a face covered with hair. In its front extremities the picture contains two unidentified objects. One is a staff and the other a ball. The hypothesis that they might be transmission antennas has been rejected."

"Can you show me the continent," I said.

He did, after a lengthy period of instruction on the computer terminal.

"And the place on the continent," I said. "If you would be so kind?"

"Oh, please (etc.)."

He showed me the continent. It looked like it always does, with the Italian boot at the bottom and the Scandinavian lion running at the top.

"And the point on the continent?"

A light dot became illuminated.

"Did you say this mystery began in 1632," I said.

"Yes, Sir, precisely," said the sergeant, who for the first time was beginning to show a real interest.

He began to turn a little red, especially in his upper body.

"King Sigismund III of Poland was buried," I said, "in 1632 in a sarcophagus in the Cracow Cathedral in the city of Wroclaw."

"Excuse me, I don't really follow you," said the sergeant.

He was already becoming quite vague, since I had definitely decided a few minutes ago to remove him and his old central sun system from the story. The last I saw was his expression of rather mild surprise when he realized that he actually existed only in the imaginary world of a creature based on the oxygen-carbon dioxide cycle. With him disappeared a shining galactic central culture, cities, memories, ancient images . . .

Separating the Living from the Dead

Winters and summers rage on all the quicker over the lakes. The clouds pass very low, and very fast. So low that you could almost touch them if you reached up.

My life is a camouflaged farmer's life, a country life. I take it with me deep into the big cities.

I have never really taken industrialization seriously. Nor capitalism either.

They are unpleasant phenomena. They will outlast my generation. My children's generation too. But they will pass. I've never doubted that a second. I've known that since the age of seven. The landscape will free itself from everything in the same way as a boy's knee frees itself from a scab.

A hawk hovering over a low-lying swamp with yellowed reeds is more real than a large airport.

Now and then I run into people who complain that the earth's resources of fossil fuels will run out. I don't regret that a moment. I find it natural.

It's a little burdensome, just like the era we live in is a little burdensome. But it will come to an end, and that is perfectly natural.

The truth about the world is not the bomber squadrons over Dresden and Hanoi. The truth about the world is not the skyscrapers in Manhattan, not that steam that billows from the subway ventilators early in the morning on Fifth Avenue. The truth about the world is a hawk hovering over a vast swamp.

It is nice to know such truths. It makes you patient. Insensitive to stabs and blows. Insusceptible even to aphasia, to language poisoning, which almost keeps you from talking, which just lets you mumble short, confused sentences like a drunk standing and leaning against a house wall.

Student turnover

41

Cultural consumer
Human resource allocation policy
Health care industry
Family planning

(You have something against my way of speaking? You don't like me to talk so much about myself? You object to my pretensions of reality? Well, *that* is what they'll give you instead. This is not a real novel, you say? What do you expect from a drunk who has just vomited up a fifth of normal prose and who stands sweating and shivering, leaning his forehead against a scarred house wall, trying to find his way back to words again?)

The woman painter Laura G. was here yesterday evening. It took her almost an hour to arrive by U-Bahn and bus. She lives on the top floor of a decaying tenement in Kreuzberg, a building not renovated this century, the third back from the street. It's like walking through Chinese boxes when you go to visit her. Yards with thin grass where signs are clearly posted in German and Turkish, forbidding children to play.

It is a strange, silent slum, completely Moslem. Silent women with black veils over their faces go up and down the stairs. You never hear a child shout, there's not a drunk in the house, men in felt slippers and with large black mustaches stealthily sneak up and down the stairs. Here, in the third building, there isn't very much sun, especially on a winter day.

The toilets form an indescribable row at the end of every corridor. Each toilet has a brown door, its own key, lattice woodwork high up on the door panel.

Laura G.'s apartment consists of a narrow hallway where visitors can't all put their coats on at the same time, a very small room, and a kitchen. The kitchen window is about one and a half feet square.

On a winter day she can't get any real sunlight for more than an hour.

This kitchen is her studio. In its halflight her paintings glow like so many marvelous precious stones. Cold foregrounds, warm

42

backgrounds like Chardin, wonderful weightless clouds hovering over blue-green, soft Renaissance landscapes.

A flying Daphne is transformed into a laurel tree, shyly pressed against the wall of an ancient temple. Her cloak falls in soft folds down a marble stairway.

For G. it is quite natural that paintings are windows. It would never occur to her to put glass over them, like the Informalists of the 1960s. She wants to have absolute transparency, so that the other world can be visible.

Ever since she was a little girl she has been sitting in rooms like this and opening her windows to the same soft Renaissance landscapes.

She comes and visits us every so often and frightens the foreign visiting research professors in the elevator. She is very dark, very tall. I think it is her eyes that frighten. She looks like one of those Russian women from the 1860s who, crouching, runs through the falling snow on Nevsky Prospekt from one cheap rental barracks to another, with a very large charge of gunpowder hidden under her coat.

Laura has no name on the art market. She is always forced to sell her canvases before she can arrange an exhibition. They hang spread out over the world, one in a villa on Lake Geneva, one in a flat in London, one in New York. Visitors stand in front of the canvases, are startled, ask who painted them. And get for an answer a name they don't know. G. doesn't make commercial products. She seeks the truth.

For the past eight months she has been working on Daphne's metamorphosis.

She arrives, very pale, very tired, very late in the evening and claims that she has been painting for exactly twenty-four hours.

"On what?"

"On the underside of a cloud."

She is the only artist I've met in my entire life who is completely serious, and in the firm conviction that it is not at all unattainable for her, she strives for perfection.

43

"If you could make a pact with the Devil," I say, "to the effect that he would obtain your soul in return for your reaching perfection, would you do it?"

"On the spot," she says.

"But you have to see to it that a couple of extra paragraphs are added," I say. "One about fame and one about fortune, about thirty million marks minimum (Picasso asked for two hundred and got it), and a productivity clause. Three canvases per day, fresh as apples.

"He'll go along with that right away. Those are just expenses. The important thing is the soul."

"What does he actually do with the souls?"

"Boil them in oil?"

"A very expensive fondue. I think he has a much more intelligent use for them. Notice that the Devil is very elitist. God seems to be interested in all souls, without discrimination; that almost suggests some sort of industrial use. The Devil is much more of a connoisseur. Strictly speaking it is very flattering to be sought out by him. Only certain souls interest him. That suggests an entirely different use. But what?"

"Notice one interesting thing. God claims all souls, against a vow that is, you might say, quite vague and generally written, at least as general as the British government's pronouncement in the Balfour Declaration. Notice that up to now God has never come and promised an artist perfection, power, and wealth, and honor in order to obtain his soul in exchange."

"Maybe things will change someday. He's had it a little too easy. We haven't been sufficiently businesslike."

"Of course, you ought to arrange a small auction in each individual case," says my wife, wisely, "that would stabilize the market.

"We've probably been duped for millennia."

"Besides," I say, "what is this talk about the Devil's evilness and God's goodness? I have the impression that we are in a—zone—where God completely controls the propaganda apparatus. But how do we know that everything people say is true? The Devil is made responsible for war, Nazism, genocide, you name it. But what is proved? You have to ask yourself: who is it that should be able to prevent war, genocide, and so on? *In whose interest* is it that we think that the Devil is responsible for everything? And the conditions in Hell? Do we have any proof at all that it really looks the way they claim? Every description I know comes from the other side. The most elementary rules of textual criticism say that you shouldn't proceed that way. You have to ask: *for whom* does Hell mean a hell, for whom does it mean an improvement? What do we know about the slums in Heaven?"

"Quiet," says my wife. "Not so loud. For such questions the walls really do have ears."

I hadn't said all this, of course, before a very peculiar sound was heard in the hall. It sounded like a light growl from a half-sleeping lion who has been disturbed by something in his dream.

"That's the refrigerator," my wife says, after a little pause in which everyone huddled around the kitchen table. The refrigerator in this apartment makes strange sounds when the thermostat clicks on.

"They ought to do something about it," I say. "For example, they ought to be able to send a study delegation, just like they do to China and Albania. And then when the study delegation comes back, they can publish an enormous report, in paperback. How do you set up a study delegation?"

The painter G. looked carefully at me with her large, dark, peculiar eyes.

"Perhaps you form a friendship society? Of course you do that. On a completely apolitical basis. The World-Inferno Friendship Society, with the mission of working for a better exchange of information, expanded cultural and theoretical contacts."

The painter's eyes were darker and more unfathomable than I had ever seen them.

"You forget that there was such a society of friends. The whole Renaissance was full of it. Things didn't go especially well for the

45

members. They were interrogated, under torture, they were burned on pyres, by the hundreds of thousands, after painful interrogation."

She surprises me at times. There are occasions when I think that she is not at all a very commonplace person.

Separating the living from the dead. Separating fantasy from reality doesn't interest me very much. Even my dreams are products of this era. But the living and the dead!

A little further out on Heerstrasse there is a sort of housing district like Tensta or Vällingby. I only go there when I'm out of pipe cleaners, and I'm always just as scared.

Five hundred to a thousand feet long, tenements thirty stories high tower up to the sky; pharmacy, grocery store, tobacco shop display themselves smartly along the square. Small children play in some sandboxes in the middle of the shopping center while their mothers are inside the stores, small children who already have small bitter faces.

My God, this is the normal world! I wonder how many such places I have seen in my life.

With a gray, rainy sky above.

Where in such a street area do you find heroes for novels?

It is no accident that all good novels are bourgeois. Novels get by without almost everything, but not without possibilities for action.

It is no trick to write a novel that begins: My uncle was head of the Third Imperial Lancers. At the time of the siege of Sebastopol . . .

A novel presupposes certain degrees of freedom, certain dimensions in which the actors can move. Balzac: money, power. A substitute is eroticism, but it doesn't go as far as you think. Eroticism ends up too easily by our being reminded of the shopping center again. Is the hero in the new suburban center the one who grows a homunculus in his bathtub? The one who

46

produces gold in the kitchen? The one who cuts up his wife and stuffs her piece by piece down the garbage disposal?

Almost the only way to get a shopping center to look like an interesting place is to depict it as a scene of a crime. But that's a lie. Here the heroes sit like nails in a wall.

But good God, a life is being lived inside these windows! Fathers of families come home from work, ask about the alarm clock that got broken in the morning, sit down with the evening newspaper . . .

The Friendship Delegation

With all the climbing up and down between buses and subways it took more than an hour for the painter G. to get home to her dark, confined apartment high up in a tenement in Kreuzberg.

It was a fairly cool evening at the beginning of April: spring had already come, but it was a tentative, fickle spring with sudden afternoon hail showers which swept away the dainty and evenly blossomed chestnut buds from the treetops.

On this day rain had fallen at dusk, then it had cleared up again, and before it became completely dark the whole sky had taken on a strange red color that was reflected on the shiny asphalt on the Strasse des 17 Juni, so that the huge, wide street looked for a moment like it had been drowned in blood.

When Laura came out onto Heerstrasse—it must have been about eleven in the evening—she had to stand and wait a rather long time at the bus stop for the 94 bus. It was already very dark, and the treetops in Grunewald right behind the bus stop moved restlessly in the night wind that had come up.

She was freezing in her thin, threadbare black coat, drew the scarf tighter around her face, and moved further inside the little Plexiglas wind shelter for the passengers at the Scholtzplatz bus stop.

The clouds dispersed, and a large, round full moon became visible in the restless sky. With her strangely blank, passionate dark eyes she looked up toward the moon, which had a strangely *haggard* look, just as if it were very tired.

When she shifted her glance down to the ground again, she discovered that she was no longer alone in the shelter. On the wooden bench sat three men who looked like they were foreigners, engaged in a lively, but very quiet, half-whispered discussion.

They must have arrived very unobtrusively.

Now the moon was shining over all of Scholtzplatz. It was hard for her to explain to herself why the strangers made a so strikingly foreign impression. They were all three very different from each other, the only thing they really had in common was that all three were very well dressed. Perhaps they were foreign professors from the Technical University's guesthouse at Heerstrasse 131?

They looked like they had outfitted themselves that very morning in some elegant boutique on Kurfürstendamm, or perhaps in New York, for their dark blue suits appeared to be American, made out of some dark, half-shiny synthetic material—occasionally when one of them moved, his suit glistened in the moonlight with an almost metallic sheen.

All three wore the exact same spring coat of Scotch tweed, carelessly tossed over their shoulders, and down on the bench, pushed in toward their unusually well-shined shoes, stood three exactly identical hard, flat attaché cases with monograms and inset locks of light metal.

"What I can't understand," thought the painter G., "is why they don't take a taxi when they are so rich. But maybe there's a shortage of taxis." At the same moment it occurred to her that maybe she didn't have any change for the bus at all, and she began to look restlessly in her purse, where only a few small coins were hidden among pawn tickets and a very worn lipstick in a shade of dark red.

At that moment she was very sure that she actually didn't have a cent for the bus (she had been expecting money for several days from a men's magazine that had promised to publish one of her graphics portraying a naked woman in its "art supplement," but it appeared as if the editors had completely forgotten her), and she had just begun to think about going back to us to borrow money for the bus, when she discovered a fifty-mark bill, brand new, lying folded up in a corner of her purse.

She was very surprised. She simply could not understand how she had been able to forget it. It must have been lying there for at least three weeks, for it was three weeks ago that she had last borrowed money from her brother.

In the firm conviction so common in gifted people that the

world really does have the duty of serving them, of being at their disposal, the painter G. slipped the bill into her hand and hoped the conductor would be kind enough to agree to change it.

Of the three foreigners, their feet and elegant hard briefcases were easiest to see, since the wind shelter's roof shaded most of the streaming moonlight from their corner, but nevertheless the face of the one sitting furthest to the left was visible.

He was a remarkably handsome, pale young man around twenty-five years old. He had a high narrow forehead with slightly protruding temples, much like a Spanish nobleman, a short black beard, and a pair of gold-rimmed glasses that gave him a learned and at the same time strong facial expression. If he hadn't looked so vaguely *foreign* he could have been a nice young assistant professor from the Free University of Berlin. "A nuclear physicist, a visiting professor at the Technical University," thought the painter G. "A brilliant young nuclear physicist who is participating in some experiments at the Technical University's new cyclotron out in Wannsee. He probably has a Spanish mother who was once a radiant Spanish beauty."

The faces of the others were not visible in the shadows.

So busy looking at the assistant professor—"His name could be Minetti, or Canetti, or Seglio," she thought to herself—so busy furtively observing the handsome young Spaniard was the painter G. that she wouldn't have noticed that the 94 had arrived and stopped at the bus stop if the three gentlemen hadn't quickly got up.

With a courtesy decidedly more foreign than Berlin they allowed her to get on first. The second gentleman looked like a small broad Englishman, rather in the style of the actor Kirk Douglas, with red hair, firm chin jutting out, very light blue eyes, and a short pointed red beard. He could have been an officer from the British occupation forces—the RAF has a large number of its officers living out on Heerstrasse—if it hadn't been that he moved with such extremely civil, relaxed movements.

The third gentleman, who was a head taller than the other

two, appeared as well to be a touch, but just a touch, older. He looked like a Polish nobleman, with a short, gray, square-clipped beard, short hair, and brown, friendly eyes. His eyelids hung like heavy sacks, and there was an expression of well-bred, mild irritation about him that made the painter G. think of an old millionaire, chairman of the board of some powerful cartel with skyscrapers in Chicago, Brussels, and Frankfurt am Main. But something didn't fit, he seemed too alive, too spiritual to have spent his time on the board and in private jets.

On the whole there was something that didn't fit, and the painter began to feel very tired, almost giddy, when she climbed up the steps to the upper deck of the bus.

She sat down in one of the front seats on the upper deck, where smoking is permitted. Besides a couple of young people in love, who were virtually twisted together and deaf to the world, and a man in a leather jacket with large doglike ears, she was alone on the upper deck of the bus.

When the conductor showed up, she still felt a little weak in her legs and hoped that she wasn't on the verge of fainting or getting sick in some way. The painter G. held out her fifty-mark bill, and the conductor grunted something incomprehensible and shook his head.

Anyone slightly familiar with Berlin knows that every bus conductor in the city would have acted in that manner. A conductor in Ankara, Stockholm, or Damascus is a servant of the public. He can be in a good or bad mood, more or less helpful and complaisant, but in principle he is a person who has the task of collecting fares and helping old women and women with baby carriages on and off the bus.

A conductor in Berlin is something entirely different.

He is a commandant. The passengers, who consist only of very poor and very old people, since everyone else takes a taxi or drives a car, are an unreliable pack that he keeps in order. He despises them, and he never talks with them other than in inarticulate grunts. Woe to the person who comes with a larger bill than ten marks! The rules state that the largest bill a conductor is obliged to change is ten marks, and he sticks to that even if his bag is bulging with bills and coins.

The painter G. knew that, she had thought about that.

She tried in any case to hand him her fifty marks with a shy little laugh.

The conductor went from a guttural grunt to a guttural roar, which meant that either she get out the fare according to the regulations or get off at the next bus stop. He didn't leave it at that, he even grabbed her by the elbow with hard bony fingers to lead her to the exit.

The painter G. didn't at all feel wronged. She was one of those people who has experienced a sufficient number of injustices of that sort in her life to accept them as a part of normal circumstances, but since she really was very tired and felt a bit ill besides, or in any case felt an unexpected dizziness, she thought:

"God, now I even have to walk, I won't get home until four A.M.! Perhaps someone here on the bus can make change for me? Perhaps the young lovers have change? Probably not. God, how this man makes me tired."

And she got ready, while the conductor's hard fingers were still on her elbow in a police grip, to go to downstairs, when one of the foreign gentlemen quite surprisingly stood up alongside of her. It was the handsome, Spanish-looking young man.

"Miss," he said, "is this man bothering you?"

Now something extremely odd happened. Before anyone, and least of all the painter G., managed to think about it, the conductor had disappeared without a trace.

But instead a frightened sparrow was fluttering around the whole upper deck of the bus, beating desperately against the windows with its wings and nearly scaring the pants off the man in the leather jacket who looked like a dog with large ears and the young people in love, who had actually awakened from their double egotism and were anxiously following what was happening.

52

Everyone began to chase the bird, which was fluttering around restlessly and hysterically between the panes, and everyone reeled back and forth as the bus lurched around curves.

Without anyone really managing to see what happened, the young Spaniard had already got the bird in his hands.

"Miss, what do you want me to do with it?"

The painter G., who found the question strange and felt pity for the poor bird, said:

"We have to let it out."

"Yes," said the handsome Spaniard, "the poor bird."

He calmly opened one of the small windows and let out the bird, which with a series of lonely peeps disappeared into the spring night.

The painter got off at Theodor-Heuss-Platz, crossed the little flat area, and went down into the subway, still a little bewildered. But the cool, springlike smell of grass after the rain soon made her feel better again. Clear moonlight shone over the whole square. In the Funk Tower the elevator was still going up and down like a little light ball on its way between sky and earth.

The three foreigners must have continued on the bus, and she felt just a slight loss, as if they had made her life a little more amusing for a moment, the whole evening's atmosphere a little more charged than it otherwise would have been.

When she went down into the U-Bahn she felt back in the familiar world again. The small green candy machines on the pillars of the subway station gave a reassuring impression, they were just the kind of objects that told you the world is neither better nor worse than it actually is, small secure details that tell you that we are still in the normal world.

A large sign with a happy swimming family was advertising vacation trips to the island of Sylt, the Deutscher Oper had a week of ballet (it occurred to her that it had been years since the last time she had the means to go to the Deutscher Oper), and some Japanese free wrestling was going to take place in the Sporthalle.

53

Then the train came in. It was a very empty train, just a few old ladies knitting here and there in the car (in Berlin you often see old ladies knitting in subway trains even at one in the morning; Berlin is a very proper city, where even tipsy youths sit very neatly in their corner speaking quietly with one another), but the first thing the painter G. noticed wasn't that but something which surprised her completely and gave her a deep feeling of unreality, the kind which makes you ask whether you are dead or alive, whether you are awake or simply dreaming.

At the far end of the car sat the three foreigners, elegantly decked out with the same rectangular briefcases propped in a row in front of their well-polished shoes.

"But that's impossible," thought the painter G. "I *saw* them continue on the bus. They should have been down at Savignyplatz by this time. Or did they get off and hop in a taxi and return and get on the subway? But there aren't any taxis that could do that in two minutes! Good God, I know that I couldn't have been on the way from the bus to the subway for more than two minutes."

The three foreigners didn't give the slightest indication of having recognized her. Two of them were engrossed in a whispered conversation about something one of them had showed the other in the *Financial Times*, the third appeared to be engrossed in a German paperback edition of Bulgakov's *The Master and Margarita*, and for a moment the painter G. toyed with the idea that the city was full of such groups of foreigners riding around in threes, with hard, rectangular briefcases and tweed overcoats nonchalantly thrown over their shoulders. "Presumably they are advertising something," she thought, and nodded off, too tired to be concerned anymore with all of the city's vagaries.

By old habit she woke up just before Turmstrasse, rubbed the sleep out of her eyes, and saw with some relief that the three foreigners were still sitting in the car, still reading and chatting quietly with each other, as the train gently slipped out of the station on its way to Kottbusser Tor.

The wind had died down completely, a faint column of smoke climbed from the large, castlelike Schultheiss brewery on Strom-strasse, and the two inner yards (where the children were not allowed to play) were bathed in the moonlight.

The painter G. shrank back in the dark archway as if expecting someone to be standing there in the shadows, but naturally there wasn't a soul around. The whole building was asleep. In Turkish, in Serbian, and in German, the heavy human bodies were tossing and turning in their sleep and dreaming dreams in three languages about distant landscapes; the small children were sucking on their rag dolls and dreaming about a place to run and play in, where no doorkeeper chased them away. A smell of sweat and cabbage soup and strange Muslim spices filled the steep winding staircase, a cat slipped softly down the steps and brushed by her knee, and when she put the key in the lock of her apartment high up under the attic and saw light coming through the keyhole, she wondered whether she had really been so careless when she left to have forgotten to turn out the light in the apartment.

At the same moment she sensed the connection, and she no longer felt surprise but just serenity, an ice-cold serenity.

The foreign gentleman who looked like an English or perhaps an Irish officer was sitting on her sofa. In front of him he had her teapot and her largest breakfast cup. Where he had gotten the warm, buttered scones which he periodically dipped into the cup with pleasure was not so easy to understand. When she left, the pantry had been empty.

The English or Irish gentleman was lazily paging through some art journals lying in front of him on the table.

From inside the narrow kitchen which served as her studio and where she had even made etchings over the gas flame a few times—a room where you could hardly turn because of the canvases, bottles of chemicals, huge clay pots stuffed full of brushes, the marble slab on which she mixed her colors, the old-fashioned easel with its wooden screws, the glass mortar she ground her colors with, corked juice bottles in which she kept her special medias, based on beeswax like the old masters—only the faucet could be heard dripping.

In the front of the easel where Daphne's metamorphosis stood and rested after the day's work were the other two foreigners. The older gentleman was smoking a cigarette in an almost femininely long amber mouthpiece, talking loudly and enthusiastically and occasionally taking such a long step backward that he hit the back of his head on the kitchen cabinet, which returned him to his former position. The other gentleman, the handsome young Spaniard, took a very contemplative attitude; he was supporting his chin in both hands and considering most carefully a detail of Daphne's cloak.

"You see what I'm saying, a remarkable painter, a master. She works like the Van Eycks, with a gray-green primer of egg-oil tempera and beeswax."

"But is it really a primer?"

"I swear! You're not going to ask me to *make a scratch* on this remarkable work of art to prove what I'm saying?"

The painter G., who by this time had been able to grasp the situation, quickly hung up her coat in the hall and stepped into the kitchen. She no longer felt tired or dizzy, she was wide awake and resolute.

"Of course you are right," she said to the older man. "I've been using an egg-oil primer, based not as you think on a beeswax medium but on a slightly more complicated one of my own invention."

"My compliments. But let me introduce our group. My name is Baal B. Zvuvim, I suggest you call me Belo, all of my friends do. These are my friends Uriel and Mr. Azaar. We are, you might say, a friendship delegation."

"I gathered that," said the painter G. "I caught on. I was thinking about roughly the same agreement as Picasso. Three paintings per day, into my nineties, fifty million dollars, three million of which in advance the first day after we sign the contract, a studio in Dahlhem—you understand that I'm really a little sick of this cramped kitchen—the fifty million to be adjusted for inflation, against the value of the 1973 dollar—of course, yes, that's roughly what I had in mind. No, there's one small supplementary clause besides."

"Oh, these small terms are a trifle for us," Belo said, and stroked his short-clipped beard. "I gladly accept the idea of indexing, but wouldn't it be just as well if we ask for a slightly larger sum, say two hundred million dollars? The prices of French castles have gone up drastically in recent years. Actually, I suggest we put the sum at two hundred and fifty. And what was that supplementary clause?"

"I would like," said the painter G., "at least for one day in my life, to be another person."

"Why?"

"Because I think in that way I would be able to learn more about history and my own life than anything else could teach me."

"Oh," said Mr. Belo. "*That* is a very difficult, complicated wish. Say, do you possibly have a glass of cold milk in the refrigerator?"

The School of Bleak

Teacups clattered pleasantly on the breakfast table. Outside the window the same weather raged as on the previous days, alternating between hailstorms and cool, hesitant sunshine.

Some plane from Hamburg must have found its way down through the morning gusts, for a poor, wet, and frozen mailman came and delivered ten days' worth of sopping Swedish newspapers, their pages stuck together.

People believe that I am maniacally interested in weather and that it is some kind of subtle symbol in my novels. As a matter of fact I hate weather, and it's not a subtle symbol at all but a simple and obvious one for what you can't do anything about and suffer from anyhow.

"I get a little upset when I read the newspapers from Sweden," my wife said. "They fight with one another so terribly."

"Papa, what's it like sitting in the rear gun turret of a Heinkel 111."

"Ask professor H. the next time he comes here. He spent half his youth in a Heinkel 111. If I understood him correctly, he didn't really enjoy it."

"That's odd," my wife said. "I've been calling the painter G. again and again, but I don't get an answer. Could she be out of town or is there something wrong with the telephone? She shouldn't be out of town."

"She probably didn't have the money to pay her bill."

"I can't understand why they fight so terribly. It's as if their horizons had narrowed, they don't have any ideas anymore, just a quarrel.

"It's like a small company that's going bankrupt, everyone waits to be laid off, everyone tramps around scolding each other, trying to find the villain.

"And the strange thing is, they can't see. There's a blind spot in their eyes. The writers can't describe it, the critics can't analyze it."

"Take it easy," I said. The consciousness of an age isn't born in five minutes. And it's not certain either that it's born in the literary pages of the newspapers. Perhaps it's in employment agency waiting rooms that the great new liberating novels are being written.

"Only shallow minds think they know a society and its secret forces in their entirety. Either it's too late to despair, or it's too early."

"Papa, why does a Messerschmitt 109 turn belly up after an attack?"

"That was a close precision fighter tactic. The Messerschmitt 109 was very strongly armored on the underside. Can't you get interested in something peaceful, young man? Why don't you build a model of a water purification plant?"

"You can't buy any models of water purification plants in the toy department."

"If the theory of productivity in *Das Kapital* is correct, the population of East Germany ought to be working three hours a day now," I said. "They don't. This is an argument that cannot be ignored. If the population of East Germany were working three hours a day, I would do everything in my power to bring about a Communist revolution. I don't see any reason to do everything in my power so that people can work eight hours a day in factories, all of which look alike, and who are persuaded besides that in doing so they enjoy some sort of special freedom or purpose.

"Nothing makes me so tired and furious as the enormous scale of lies that today's world contains. And when people realize how great the lies really are, a storm will blow in that will not only sweep away capitalism and East European state capitalism—it will sweep away industrialism in its entirety."

"You're beginning to talk like John Ruskin more and more every day."

"Note that I don't think industrialism will be done away with through stenciled handbills and pamphlets. It will do away with itself. Through suffocation, through self-poisoning. Through loss of energy. It is not capitalism that governs us. It is technology itself.

"Every revolutionary society in the twentieth century up to now has simply created a poor copy of the previous one. The Palace of Culture in Warsaw is a poor copy of the skyscrapers in Manhattan. Russian Tobaljev or French Concorde, it's all the same to me. Evil runs deeper than anyone believes. That's the simple truth, and until it becomes common knowledge, I don't understand what good there is in preaching about Judgment Day."

"Preaching about Judgment Day! Are you going to talk that way? If anyone heard you, you'd make enemies."

"That's beside the point. It's not my job to go around being popular. Television talkshow hosts like Lennart Hyland can go around being popular. A serious person avoids popularity and is satisfied with only a few friends and enemies."

"Are you sure there's something wrong with G.'s telephone?"

"It could be that she's out of town."

"Your political analyses get stranger every day."

"I really like believing, I really like being with people where everyone thinks I'm right, but my desire for knowledge is greater than my love of pleasure."

"Do you want another cup of tea?"

"   "

"Why don't you answer? What are you thinking about?"

"I'm thinking about King Sigismund III of Poland. He's buried in Cracow's cathedral. I saw the sarcophagus there once. And then I'm thinking about a school of fish."

"If you ask people what they're thinking about, and really get a candid answer, it always strikes you that they think about such strange things."

"No thanks. I don't want any more tea. If you drink too much tea you can get hallucinations."

"What sort of a school of fish do you mean?"

"I'm thinking about a school of bleak."

"A school of bleak?"

"Yes. Off the eastern bank over the shallows in Lake Norra Nadden, one summer afternoon in my childhood. The shallow water is full of brown, round stones, flattened and made oval from the water's grinding movements, and the water is crystal clear. That's where the school of bleak is. If you make the slightest movement it disappears like a shadow, like something spiritual, immaterial, with a silver luster."

"Really?"

"It took me almost thirty years until I realized how exotic that experience was. How many children do you think there are in the big cities of Europe or America, or in country towns for that matter, who have the chance to experience something similar? It's nice to sit along the shore of a lake as a child. A small, brownish, Västmanland lake like that is a good teacher. You don't believe in every piece of nonsense when you've had such a teacher as a child."

"What do you mean?"

"I mean just that."

"But what do you *mean*?"

"Take it, for example, as an erotic picture. Someone who has seen such a school of bleak come and then disappear cannot be lured into believing there exist any erotic techniques. No more than there is any way guaranteed to help you have ideas. Either they come, or they don't."

"What else are you thinking about?"

"About a comic-strip clipping on an outhouse. An evil old ruler of a distant planet trying to prevent a nice young couple from breaking out of a strangely formed glass sphere. What's really happening in the picture?"

"Perhaps it's just the opposite. Not someone trying to prevent people from getting out but trying to drive them out of Paradise. The picture represents Adam and Eve driven out of Paradise by the angel."

AND THEN ONCE MORE; TELEPHONE CONVERSATION FROM SWEDEN

Pedestrian laws, university reforms, left-wing groups chewing one another up like dogs who chew up their masters' slippers. Blind teenage idols singing in churches. The ditches in central Stockholm being filled with parking spaces. The Bilderberg Group meeting in Lidingö. The myth about the secret society beneath society grows rampant. Conspiracies revealed. In employment office waiting rooms the novels of the era are written. In the fields wrecked autos are rusting. And everything in a very impersonal, very uninteresting way.

THOSE SCHOOLS OF BLEAK

They're connected with Paradise. Paradise consists of shimmering silver bleak in shallow water. In Paradise souls move like shimmering silver fish in shallow water. For me they are connected with Franz Berwald's *Symfonie singulière* played over white water on a night in June at the sixtieth parallel—Berwald played over fields of cotton grass, played over humus-scented water. Almquist's Tintomara moves quietly among the opera house stage settings and leaves a scent of the forest.

And the smell of lilacs, lilac arbors at the corners of old farmhouses, and white dust from the roads, and the old people, the ones that died around 1950, who still talked about "The German," about "The Russian" when they discussed the radio reports from the Second World War, sitting in their lilac arbors. (The Swedish world champion runner Gunder Hägg competes against the American Dries, and everyone is listening in the arbors.)

Yes, you're right. I am one of those who at age thirty-seven is already beginning to think that the world must have once been very much better than it is now—Heaven, the myth of Paradise.

Of course, it's childhood that begins to haunt, the experience of an age when you had the power to have much stronger, much crazier, much more perverse wishes than now.

It wasn't a happier age, but it feels happier in retrospect, since you had the ability to imagine much greater, much more radical forms of happiness.

The know-it-alls write in the newspapers and ask what we really need art for. What do we need art for? A trumpet phrase of Stravinsky, an extremely dissonant chord of Gesualdo, a Berlioz horn passage that laughs, the tress in Botticelli's portrait of Simonetta Vespucci . . . Good God, yes, what do we need beauty for? To remind us of what we are, of course. To remind us of childhood. To remind us of childhood's blind, sensible hunger to be ourselves.

My God, who was the idiot who first figured that the highest thing in life is to sacrifice yourself for the collective? During its long history Europe has had a single intellectual virtue, which is that, time after time, its philosophers, authors, painters, and composers have reminded us that we are individuals.

In other words: reminded us of our real dimensions, reminded us of our childhood.

When I was seven I sat perched on a beam high up under the roof in a barn. It was at least thirteen feet down to the floor.

"You wouldn't dare jump," said my malicious little playmates standing down below, as tiny as coins with their white faces directed up into the semidarkness. "You wouldn't dare jump. You'd kill yourself."

"But I *want* to jump," I said.

And jump I did. Just that nobody had noticed an old bucksaw that sat there in the semidarkness and could quite easily have killed me, if it hadn't been that it only gouged a very impressive gash in my right thigh from which the blood spurted.

I took it quite calmly, and at that time they seldom put stitches in wounds that could heal by themselves. I knew you always had to pay.

But, and this is important, I didn't jump to satisfy the expectant

63

little faces of the collective down there in the darkness. I jumped because it was my own way of telling myself that life is magnificent and just how magnificent only I knew.

NEVER BEFORE OR AFTER HAVE WE HAD IT SO GOOD AS IN THE FIFTIES

my father often says. The Korean boom, taxes still relatively reasonable, decent monetary value, rents you could put up with. Some time in 1952 he bought a motorcycle, a 125 cc Husqvarna, and though I was supposedly too young to drive it, I helped him break it in. It took a little while to figure out the gearshift, but then it was fantastic to roar along, fifteen years old, completely illegally, on the highway at sixty miles an hour and feel the wind rush against me, the Renaissance wind,
the same wind,
in principle,
that blows in Monteverdi's operas.

WHY DIDN'T I CONTINUE TO LIVE THAT WAY?

The Story of Uncle Stig

Cleverness, naturally. Cleverness hindered me. You can't live like that if at the same time you want to be clever and be admired for your cleverness.

In our family cleverness is epidemic. We always push it a touch *too* far. We find out early on that we are clever, people make a little room in the ecological niche for us and resign themselves to our being that way, and then of course we immediately have to become a little more clever, and it isn't long before we are completely fanatical in our cleverness.

(The other day I was sitting and counting, and I realized that I have written over twenty books in just over a decade without thinking what a *terribly* bad impression that makes in a refined, inhibited, sensitive country like Sweden, where poetry and spirituality have always been "closely related to silence.")

That's no good. You should be clever, but in moderation.

In our family cleverness always evolves into a catastrophe in the same way.

I'm sure that I'm the ninth or tenth case.

Uncle Stig is a good example.

If I remember correctly, he began as a regular corporal in the Horse Guard, but that's so long ago that no one has a really clear idea of what he was doing there. This much is clear, he didn't quite get promoted to highest in command, and I'm convinced that at heart it irritated him very much. He didn't like the Horse Guard following that blunder on their part, and afterward he actually became a Communist for a couple of decades, at a time when it wasn't really opportune to be one. I remember that he had a subscription to Stalin's works at the time of the Communist coup in Prague; he didn't just subscribe, he read them and liked them.

I remember a really nice walk in the country in northern Västmanland in 1947 when we saw a glowworm—it was the first time in my life that I had seen a glowworm, a little green dot moving along the roadside that we carefully put into the grass so that it wouldn't get run over—and he tried to convince me that Stalin's philosophical writings were the highest expression of man's millennium-long struggle, and I tried to convince him that he was wrong, the highest expression of man's centuries-long struggle was as a matter of fact not Stalin's thought at all but Gustav Mahler's Seventh Symphony.

In 1947 I went through one of my great decadent periods and loved everything that was beautiful, dedicated to death, and spiritual.

Starting with such a difference of opinion, you can't become anything other than friends.

I did my best to convince him that there wasn't any deep antithesis between Stalinism and the death wish (I suspect that I was absolutely right), and he did his best to convince me that there was no antithesis between Stalinist principles in musical culture and Gustav Mahler's symphonies (that was just when Stalin's anti-Semitism was on the verge of seriously bursting forth, but it could be that Uncle Stig was right in any case), and I have a clear recollection that the walk surprised both of us. Neither of us had really thought that there could be so many strange opinions in the world, and neither of us had any really good way of confronting someone else's opinions. So we declared that they were completely compatible and continued to look for glowworms.

Much earlier, right after the Horse Guards, Uncle Stig had begun to develop his special talent.

He was an inventor. He lived in a tenement and for the most part had his workshop in the kitchen, and that led to a number of problems with the neighbors, since he lived in a poorly sound-proofed one-room apartment, but he didn't give a damn.

From his apartment inventions flowed out into the world for two decades.

66

He was a regular visitor at the Patent Office, his lawsuits against various licensees kept a couple divisions of the Stockholm Magistrate's Court continuously occupied; for however he wrote his license agreements he was always swindled out of the entire invention when it came down to the bottom line.

Take, for example, the time he became interested in water faucets!

He came up with various ingenious quick connectors of the sort that are used when you fit the hose of the washing machine to the faucet in the kitchen or the garden hose to the tap in the garden.

There are probably twenty such quick connectors on the market, and at least fifteen of them go back to Uncle Stig's kitchen workshop in Söder. No matter what he did there was always someone who snatched the patent from him at the last second, and he was ordered to pay all of the legal costs besides. No wonder Uncle Stig was a Stalinist! I'd have become a Wagnerian for less!

It always began with some elegant gentleman in an American luxury car driving onto his street in Söder and groping their way up the stairway, through baby carriages and snot-nose kids and the smell of cabbage soup, and ringing at his door. Some clatter was heard while Uncle Stig moved things away—he always had quite a few things standing in the hall, things piled up there—then they made their way into his kitchen, and sat down on the kitchen sofa while my uncle soberly filed away with an awful noise on some complicated piece of work at the sink.

After a half hour or so he would pretend that he had noticed them and ask what they wanted, and it always turned out that his inventive activity had come to their attention and that they wanted to form a consortium to launch his inventions once and for all.

Since Uncle Stig loathed business in general and capitalists in particular, he invariably went along with them.

He would get a few thousand in advance, and with their cases full of revolutionary quick connectors and faucets the gentlemen marched out into the world. It took a year or two before he discovered that there was a mass of his connectors under foreign patent, bringing in millions to the patent owners. He himself continued to stumble through Engels' *Anti-Dühring* and find new areas for evidence of the *Weltgeist*.

Baby carriages that could go up steps, padlock designs, can-openers you couldn't hurt yourself on—God only knows what he brought forth out of the depths of nothingness and turned into amazing realities.

At that time, right after the war, there weren't many cars on the streets, not many motor vehicles at all. Imports hadn't really got going yet. And the country was still full of bicyclists who crowded the streets outside the factory areas at five o'clock every afternoon.

Uncle Stig had long had his eye on the bicycle.

"Remember, little friend," he used to say to me, "your uncle will go down in history as the man who perfected the bicycle."

His theory was absolutely sound. Sooner or later, he reasoned, the time will come when the earth's fossil fuels will be at an end. Then we would see which inventions were temporary whims of fashion and which had the future before them. The automobile is typical of the ones that will disappear. The airplane, too. The wheelbarrow is the type of real invention that can be used as long as you like. Originally invented by a Chinese general so that soldiers could more easily transport their gear during long marches, it has proved to be one of the best and most durable inventions of all time, a simple lever whose fulcrum continually moves forward, thus relieving the carrier or lifter.

Another example of an invention that will be around forever is the hot-air balloon. A flying machine that nothing in the world can really prevent from flying, so long as the art of weaving and varnishing a piece of silk is known.

A third example of a truly great invention is the bicycle. Our

68

automobiles, buses, and trucks are really nothing other than disguised velocipedes, temporarily adapted to fossil fuels; they will disappear about as quickly as they came.

But the bicycle will remain, it will last for thousands of years.

"Therefore, it's time we do something for it," said Uncle Stig.

The bicycle was the field in which he wanted to fully express his cleverness.

He thought about the bicycle for years.

He didn't talk very much to us about it until around 1947, when some of his theories began to mature.

"It's absolutely absurd," he said, "that no one has figured out that a bicycle can of course compete very well in speed with a car. It's just a question of the distribution of forces."

On Uncle Stig's bicycle there would be no idiotic air resistance. So he put the cyclist in a prone position using a complicated system of elbow and thigh supports, with his face behind a little windshield. Which meant the cyclist needed a little help from his friends to get on and off the bicycle and that it might not be so easy to stop at red lights, but good God, at that time there were hardly any red lights other than at the main intersection in downtown Stockholm, and so it didn't matter so much.

Of course the pedals had to be moved up to a suitable height, about where the basket sits on a normal bicycle.

"A typical absurdity," said Uncle Stig, "that the power of the leg is only used during a third of the pedal stroke on a normal bicycle. The power should naturally be distributed equally throughout the entire stroke."

So he slipped the cyclist's feet into a couple of solid leather straps, mounted two driving gears, with separate chains, one for each foot. He made them elliptical, for reasons so complicated that I cannot explain them here, and placed the ellipses against each other.

A bicycle like that is a little hard to get going. So he equipped it with a gearbox with at least fifteen different speeds. The largest gearwheel was as big as a dessert plate and the smallest as small as a two-öre piece.

The handlebars looked rather impressive with all their grips and paraphernalia when he showed them to us in his kitchen one Sunday in March of 1949. In front of his nose the pilot, or whatever you want to call him—the cyclist, the test driver—had a rather large, substantial speedometer.

When he showed us the test model, it struck us that the speedometer went up to ninety miles an hour.

"Isn't that a little high?" we said.

"That may not be adequate," said Uncle Stig. "No one can tell how fast this bicycle will be able to go. At very high speeds new aerodynamics will come into play. No one knows what effect they will have. Note that no human being has ever traveled at such speeds by means of his own leg power."

"Yes they have," I said.

"Who," Uncle Stig said, incensed.

"The ones who jump off the Katarina elevator over Mosebacke."

"Hm."

The wheels were very narrow. It was a converted racing bicycle without fenders and with those narrow tires you can slip on and off in a second. The steering, apart from the elbow supports, was the usual down-curving racers' handlebars. It probably weighed around fifty-five pounds, and the gearshift eleven, with all its chains and gears and gadgets. I seriously considered asking to test-drive it, but I understood he would never have allowed that, and we were in his kitchen besides.

On the first Sunday in April of 1949 the test run took place out on Södertälje Road, which at that time didn't have much traffic.

I wasn't there myself, but I've heard a great deal about it.

He had sent out a letter to the press and invited the *Ny Dag, Morgon-Tidningen*, and *Afton-Tidningen*, but I don't know whether any newspaper people came at all. I never found any articles in the papers.

It was a slightly hazy April morning, like April mornings at that latitude often are.

The test model was brought out to the starting line—I don't know exactly where it was—by taxi. The bicycle turned out to have a tiny red pennant with hammer and sickle hanging on a separate little stick from the handlebars, and perhaps that is what made it unpopular among some of the newspapers.

Gathered there were a few friends, party comrades, old cronies, a few relatives, and a girl whom Uncle Stig knew.

Most of his cronies were from the Sofia Bicycle Club, where Uncle Stig had always had a few friends.

Uncle Stig—dressed in honor of the occasion in gym shoes, gym shorts, the Sofia Bicycle Club jersey, leather cap, and thick driving goggles—supervised the unloading of the bicycle and paid the taxi. The driver got a little surly when he didn't get much of a tip, hardly five percent.

Uncle Stig made a short speech to those gathered:

Comrades!

You are present at a historic occasion, the first attempt to attain a speed of seventy-five miles an hour on a bicycle. I know that my bicycle ought to be able to reach higher speeds, but I don't know how high a speed the rims will take. Therefore I will limit my test this time to seventy-five miles an hour. If I succeed it will be a step forward for humanity, for socialism, for peace in the world, since my invention is for the service of peace. If I fail others will take up my fallen torch.

My test model, which you see here—the result of years of hard work under adverse external circumstances—means a step toward the future, toward that future when the struggle over disappearing fuel supplies on earth will jeopardize world peace. My invention will help protect this peace. It would never have come into being had it not been for the interest taken by my old comrades at the Sofia Bicycle Club.

So my test bicycle is called *Joseph Sofia*.

Now I must ask two men to help me get going. Forward! For World Peace!

A somewhat dry open-air applause followed these words.

Several people pointed out in passing that Uncle Stig had always been a little ludicrous. A few younger members among the groups represented made fun of the machine.

Some uncontrolled laughter and chatter arose here and there in the circle of spectators, but then quieted down. It was still a long time to the Twentieth Party Congress.

An ice-cold rain brought with it substantial gusts of wind. It was really a dreadfully cold morning, and everyone realized things better get moving.

A couple of old-timers from the Sofia Bicycle Club disappeared down the road on their bicycles. The idea was that they would hear the starting gun in the air and start their watches so as to measure the speed after one, two, and three thousand yards and record this record attempt.

Uncle Stig straightened his socks, two of his friends from the Sofia Club lifted him up and placed him in the complicated system of arm, thigh, and stomach supports that formed the saddle. It almost looked like when you lift an inboard motor into a boat.

The abdominal strap was buckled on, the feet fixed to the pedals.

"How do you get off?" someone said.

"I reduce the speed and loosen the strap, of course," said Uncle Stig, and it was so obvious an answer that everyone actually began to realize they were a little slow not to have been able to come up with such a simple solution themselves.

Still, everyone felt uncomfortable somehow. As he lay there, fastened around the stomach and feet in his gleaming device, he looked like a prisoner of progress, absolutely fettered to his shining machine.

"Production exists for the sake of mankind and not mankind for production," an old character said, a bearded pacifist in steel-rimmed glasses in the rear of the circle of spectators. But he quieted down.

"It's never going to work," said the girl friend of one of his friends in the Sofia Bicycle Club. She wasn't a member herself, but she had the job of minding the coffee thermos.

But they got him moving. It appeared it wasn't especially easy to keep a balance on such a monster of a bicycle, particularly at the beginning, before it had got up some speed. Uncle Stig practically swerved from one side of the road to the other, but then he had gathered so much speed on his tough-pedaling bicycle that he could shift to the next gear—and suddenly he was on his way, the speedometer creeping up slowly, slowly, in front of his nose, to three, four, five, six miles an hour.

Because of the number of gears, it gathered speed more slowly at first than a normal bicycle, and Uncle Stig was already sweating even though it was windy and cold.

He discovered that it actually makes a great difference if the foot has to pedal the entire revolution.

Then he was out on the stretch, and then he was going faster and faster, the chain jumping cheerfully from one gear on the shaft to the next.

The wind began to rush around him,
the wind.

In one minute from four miles an hour to forty, that's not so bad!

An occasional unevenness in the road surface almost caused the bicycle to lift up, a bicycle of sixty-six pounds with a rider weighing one hundred and thirty-two—that is to say, one hundred and ninety-eight pounds in all isn't exactly the same at forty miles an hour as a car weighing over a ton.

73

The wind,
a Monteverdi wind,
a freedom wind,
increased every second, and the needle of the speedometer rushed
upward to ever more unbelievable numbers.

Aha, the first car appeared! It was a rather heavily loaded
gravel truck, but in any case a vehicle. It must have been going
around forty-five miles an hour.

Uncle Stig passed it as easily as a shadow, like a breath of
wind, and he saw in the rearview mirror how the driver swerved
precariously trying to collect himself behind the wheel after the
shock.

Fifty miles an hour, the bicycle makes long leaps at each bend
in the road, still not tiring in the least, and the needle is still
creeping upward and the falling rain is no longer a cold but
cooling rain, and the Monteverdi wind rushes past around him
full of mysterious promises, and the prisoner of progress is
completely free inside the glass bubble of his progress, his inspi-
ration, his cleverness

AND THE RAIN WASHES AWAY DECADES OF WEARI-
NESS

the wind is already a storm, and it is sixty miles an hour, *sixty*!
and he passes two automobiles, hardly noticing the smell of
gasoline, and they too swerve madly at having been passed and

THE TIMERS WHIRL BY WITH PALE FACES

at seventy miles an hour a squall hits and throws *Joseph Sofia*
and its death-defying driver in a huge arc out over the fields, and
it took him three months in the hospital for the bone in his thigh
to come close to healing, and all the old retired people in the beds
alongside almost laughed themselves to death when they heard
about what had happened to him, and he got well again, very well

74

even, but he never made any inventions again, and he put on a little weight and became calmer and talked more quietly about Stalinism and eventually bought himself a row house in Hägersten, and when you saw him walking around pushing his lawnmower, a very fat and silent two-bit engineer with Stalin's philosophical work stowed away in the attic, you could, of course, see that somewhere something must have gone wrong, though it wasn't easy to say what it was, but it had really gone awry somewhere—his life had, so to speak, culminated—and the tulips grew in his yard, and the grass became greener and greener every year

AND SOMEWHERE EVERYTHING HAD GONE WRONG

and that's the end of the story about cleverness.

An Intergalactic War II

The huge parabolic dish antennas on the planet Ygal-Ygal, four or five miles from one side to the other, moved nervously from one sector of the sky to another.

The weak, deep-red twilight from the old dying sun Ham-Ofad could barely cast shadows from the strange, wind-polished boulders in the stark desert. For two years it has been afternoon on the planet, and a fresh southwesterly breeze of –120 degrees Celsius with an average wind velocity of eight hundred feet per second swept over the surface. Not a speck of dust in this desert moved, the obvious explanation being that its mass was around thirty to forty tons.

Ygal-Ygal is an unusually large planet, especially with respect to proportions in our galaxy. In this seemingly uninteresting red desert in twilight, where the horizon seems to lie hundreds of miles away, even extremely experienced space geologists from ancient civilizations could have noticed a thing or two to make them open their eyes wide.

And not without reason. Ygal-Ygal is no ordinary giant planet.

As a matter of fact it's not in our galaxy at all.

Kiirk-Fa didn't bother in the least to brake when he came into Ygal-Ygal's atmosphere. On the contrary he closed his short, aggressively shaped wings and let himself fall thousands of feet into the planet's interior. His short, impertinent beak split the great mass of stone floating by him like a cool wind, a Monteverdi wind, and with a crash as if of a thousand blockbusters he let himself fall sensually through the granite. The fresh wind of crystallized stone, the feeling of finding himself again in the harsh and secure landscape of his home territory put him in an excellent humor. He narrowly avoided colliding with another Blip who was slowly and leisurely circling upward through the stone mass. Like men they exchanged harsh, manly greetings, and each continued on his own way.

With a deceleration that would have turned a falling meteor into bright gas plasma in one second, the city's outer magnetic field caught him, and in an elegant glide he crashed through the institution's wall.

"Welcome!"

"Welcome, Kiirk-Fa!"

"Welcome!"

"Yes. Too bad. The signals are the same. All our attempts to break it have failed."

"Are you in contact, Docent?" (I am translating a title that is, perhaps, not quite right to translate as "docent." Some translators might prefer "private docent," taking into account some social relationship on Ygal-Ygal that is difficult to understand, others again might choose "little sister," but I can't get involved in that, otherwise I'd never get to the point of my story.)

Kiirk-Fa shook a little granite dust out of his wings with some short energetic flaps.

Blips are born in stone, live in stone, and fly in stone like our skylarks in spring air. Nevertheless they seem to have an ancient, deeply rooted aversion to becoming dusty.

"Just fragmentary, Chief Researcher. There have been an unusual amount of intergalactic disturbances the past few days. That complicates the time shifts."

"I understand, Docent. Can you turn it up a bit, Docent?"

"Certainly."

The docent wisped a violet ring hanging with phosphorescent light in the middle of the room's granite darkness.

"A little louder, please, I guess I'm a little hard of hearing from the landing. I've been out in empty space too long."

Obligingly the docent wisped the ring once more.

VIVAT ET FLOREAT REX

sang out the loudspeaker in three voices, a red, glowing plasma on the ceiling.

"That doesn't tell me anything," said Kiirk-Fa.

77

"It didn't tell me anything the other times either. But our intelligence division in System 203 has explained it. It is Adam Jarzebsky."

"Damn," said Chief Researcher Kiirk-Fa. "*Damn!* That's his court composer."

The docent nodded.

"Deadlock again. Paralysis! Damnation!"

"Yes, Chief Researcher, it seems as if he controls the fleet. That's not so hot either!"

"But what the hell does he want with it?"

"If we only knew."

"Can you call Division A, Docent?"

"Certainly."

"There's only one way out."

"And what would that be?"

"*Infiltration.* Division A has to help us smuggle in a spy. By whatever means. A spy."

Turned up to a volume that would have made an armada of jet planes starting sound like a whisper, with abnormally crude silver trumpets, Adam Jarzebsky's ancient solemn hymn to King Sigismund, "*Vivat et Floreat Rex*," was heard through a space that wasn't quite so empty at all.

The Painter G. Makes a Decision

"It ought to be later in the evening, but the clock has actually been at one for an hour," thought the painter G.

The teacups clattered pleasantly in her workroom. The extremely weak ray of red, the first sign of a spring morning approaching the horizon, had been hanging completely still for an hour, or was it more.

Those gentlemen, Belo, Uriel, and Azaar, sat lined up on the couch under the bookshelf, like well-bred young diplomats from an underdeveloped country invited to a cocktail party in Bonn, and looked at the painter with love.

Hadn't she become prettier in the last half hour? Weren't her eyes shining with a new, deeper luster?

"Dear Laura," said Belo (they had agreed to call each other Laura and Belo), "I think all of the small points can be cleared up very easily. A studio in Grunewald, some tens of millions of dollars in cash, and the rest in monthly payments, indexed for inflation. World renown and, finally, artistic perfection, which, however, is a significantly more difficult matter.

"There is really only one of your stipulations which bothers me, and that is this idea that it is necessary for you to become another person for twenty-four hours, at a point in time chosen by you.

"You understand that isn't the normal contract."

"But Belo, you've heard my reasons?"

"I've heard your reasons, and I have great sympathy for them. I think you would actually gain more knowledge that way than any other way that is at a person's disposal during her lifetime. It's just that your request is a little unusual. It puts our resources to an extraordinary test."

"But Belo, think of the price, you'll get my soul, my immortal soul forever."

(She couldn't stop her voice from trembling a bit when she uttered those words.)

Belo leaned back in the couch and looked at his two colleagues for a moment with a certain weary resignation.

"Laura, you are a smart woman, a very smart woman. Therefore, there is all the reason in the world to talk frankly with you. You have a clear and good mind, your heart is in the right place, you are a wonderful painter, and before you are done," he closed his eyes for a moment and leaned back contemplatively in the couch much like someone reminded of a pleasant memory, "the world's great museums will fight like madmen over your canvases. There will come a time when a little silver pencil drawing of yours will go for fifty thousand marks at Sotheby's in London. But you understand, dear Laura," for a moment he let a paternal hand rest on her arm, and Laura drew it back, startled, as an unexpectedly sensual warmth spread through her wool sweater, "in spite of everything your experience is limited."

"Of course," said Laura, a bit surly.

"Yes, it is limited," continued Belo paternally, "and you have to understand that. You say that 'we' will 'get' your 'immortal soul,' and I suspect that you associate the most unpleasant ideas with these words. What you don't perceive is that you are letting two thousand years of hostile propaganda speak through your language. Without being conscious of it yourself, you speak a language that is completely infiltrated by hatred, endless hatred of us, of our social system, of our forms of life, of everything we stand for." For a moment he seemed genuinely moved, but he quickly resumed his avuncular, professorial tone. "You say that 'we' will 'get' your 'immortal soul.'"

"Which 'we'?" added Uriel.

"Precisely. Which 'we'? And what do you mean by 'get'? I can imagine exactly what ideas you associate with this. Huge oceans of boiling sulfur, rains of blood, lizardlike monsters that make dreadful, shameless passes at you, lizards with human bodies that insist on licking the noblest parts of your body with their rough tongues, abominable flying monsters that pursue you through

80

one-hundred-degree deserts where you walk up to your calves through boiling lead, disgusting old women with insidious smiles who try to stick out your eyes with hatpins . . .

"Belo," said Uriel, "try to curb your fantasy, can't you see she's very pale?"

"Excuse me," said Belo. "I only wanted to give some examples of what has been said about us through the millennia. But only, of course, to illustrate what disgusting propagandistic lies have been spread about us."

"Can one really be sure they are lies," said Laura. "Think of Hieronymus Bosch and Pieter Brueghel and . . ."

"Dear Laura," and only at the last moment could he suppress an impulse to put a paternal hand on her upper arm once more, "let me once and for all point out that they are lies. Crude, brilliantly conducted, persistent, systematic lying propaganda.

"Don't forget that the same people who spread these lies did not shy away from burning hundreds of thousands of young women like you at the stake, piercing Cathari on poles, drowning Anabaptists in rivers, wringing confessions out of children in Dalarna (a Scandinavian province) with glowing tongs. And what did the children confess? That they had been offered sweets!

"From such people, you must realize, you cannot expect accurate information about a foreign world."

Laura nodded slightly, but still looked so pale that Azaar in a brotherly gesture wiped his handkerchief quickly across her brow—that upset her a bit, for she had just been thinking that he really *was* an unusually handsome man—and offered to fetch her a glass of whiskey, which she declined, knowing full well that she hadn't had the money to buy any whiskey in months. Mr. Azaar didn't settle for that but quickly took out a pocket flask of Haig & Haig from his elegant briefcase, and the painter G. noticed in passing that it must have been purchased in the duty-free liquor shop at the airport in Frankfurt am Main.

Uriel went obediently to the kitchen and got glasses, and the mood, somewhat tense for a moment, lightened quickly when the smell of choice whiskey spread around the room. Did Haig & Haig really taste so good?

"What I wanted to say," continued Belo, relieved, "is that it isn't at all a question of someone wanting to drown you in a sea of blood or boil you in sulfur. We are quite simply another world system, another empire. For a very long time we have been in an uneven and hard struggle which has gradually developed into a fragile balance of terror between the powers that normally rule this planet.

"It is a hard, unsentimental war in which the means are not always the prettiest, I can promise you. Agents infiltrate from both sides. It is a dirty, hard, cold job, with both sides fulfilling their duty without sentimentality whatsoever.

"But this I can promise you—there is no question of sulfurous lakes. Nor is anyone out to 'get' your soul. Those are just ideas you have from childhood, when you lie in the dark, waiting for someone to come and 'take' you, right?"

He had talked so long and so eagerly that he almost lost his breath. Uriel took over almost without interruption, and with the same, slightly weary voice as if he had explained the same thing over and over again hundreds of times.

"It's not a question of that, it's a question of attracting certain—talents—who can be of future use to us and who can work and live with us forever. We are somewhat elitist in our selection, owing to the fact that we have never been as interested in mass appeal. We are a powerful empire. Our way of arranging things, our entire system, is rather unlike anything here. It is quite possible that a newcomer will have difficulty adapting, that he or she will miss one thing or another which he or she is used to, and that the newcomer will find this or that new and strange. But there isn't any question of lakes of sulfur, other than the possibility of some remote nature preserve, and if so, only as a point of interest for tourist excursions.

82

"What we are after is your work, your talent, dear Laura, nothing else. And that implies, you understand, that the price you pay is not at all as high as you imagine, sitting here, misled as you are by millennia of frightening propaganda."

"I understand," said Laura. "But how can I be sure you're telling the truth?"

"You usually rely on the words of an honorable man," said Belo. "As Uriel here said, the price you pay isn't at all so frightfully high as you think, and that makes this business of your unusual additional stipulation seem a little strong.

"Of course, it is entirely correct that you will be spending eternity in a place that for all future time will prevent you from the possibility of spending it elsewhere. But in the first place, you have to be somewhere in eternity and, in the second place, you can't be entirely certain, either, that the other place is as wonderful as the many thousand years of lying propaganda maintain.

"Frankly speaking, I think you should refrain from jacking up the price unnecessarily and join now."

The painter G. leaned back in her chair. The clock stood still at one, and the red streak on the horizon hadn't become any wider.

"It's funny," she said, "but as long as I was thinking of sulfur lakes and rains of blood and those—lascivious—lizards, the whole matter seemed completely settled. But now when you say that it isn't so dangerous, I begin to think of shopping lines, and the smell of cheap washing detergent, and bureaucratic forms that have to be filled out, and crowded buses you have to stand in line for in the sleet, and then it's not so tempting anymore.

"How's the climate? It's at least not damp and cold?"

Belo, who had been watching her lovingly during the past few minutes, gave a start, as if he just now had become conscious of what she was talking about.

"The climate? Of course, the climate. Well, it's a very large continent, larger than both Asia and Africa together, there are all sorts of climates. You'll probably settle in some place where the climate suits you. Clearly there are a few places that have some-what extreme conditions, and it may turn out that not everything is lying propaganda but a good part of the stories are based on medieval travelers' overexcited ideas about what they saw. For the most part, though, I'm convinced you'll have no difficulty at all adapting to the climate and that you'll find a place where the air is warm and dry and spring comes early."

"That's funny," said the painter G., "but with everything you say I become more uncertain."

At the same moment she noticed something. It had become lighter in the room. The red streak on the eastern horizon had grown noticeably: the distinct ticking of the clock was again heard in the room. And suddenly it was three-thirty in the morning.

The painter G. felt very tired. The ticking suddenly seemed so loud that she wondered how the neighbors were on the whole able to sleep through it.

The gentleman who asked to be called Belo got up from the couch with a certain heaviness.

"Okay," he said. "Our delegation is in principle not a team of negotiators but a friendship delegation."

"And so what," said the painter G.

"I see no solution other than your coming with us for a week and getting some idea of the situation yourself before we enter into any agreement."

"But can that be done?"

"Of course it can, my child. We have nothing to conceal. On the contrary, we are eager for cultural contacts to be expanded."

"Is there anything I need to take with me?" G. asked nervously.

"Yes, a toothbrush and perhaps a change of clothes—and a warm sweater. The evenings in certain regions can be a little cool."

"But can I be sure of coming back?"

"Of course. We don't make it a habit to go and lose members of friendship delegations," said Belo, a bit hurt.

84

"Okay. I'll take a look. Just wait so I can leave a note for the landlady to water my plants. Are you saying we're going to start right away?"

"As soon as possible! We have to be on our way before the sun comes up."

"Hold on, I'll just get a slip of paper. It seems as if someone is always stealing my pencils."

The Shower of Shot, Captured in Flight in Front of the Hunter's Gun

It's been afternoon for a couple of months.

This fact expressed itself in various ways.

I moved to Scholtzplatz. Scholtzplatz lies a bit further out in Berlin, a stone's throw from Spandau, a corner, the roughest, but still, a corner of the great Grunewald forest, where merry horsemen ride forth and the beeches were becoming greener by the day.

A light mist lay over Berlin.

I left without regrets the huge apartment in Schöneberg, with its sudden cold gusts of wind from the closets and its retired army surgeons and little sharp-beaked colonels' wives on the upper floors, and squeezed myself and my family into a comfortable little three-room place out at Scholtzplatz.

I like suburbs. I always have. From the window at Scholtzplatz I could see a bus stop and two strangely shaped pines.

They reminded me of Väster Våla, especially when large rain clouds passed behind them.

My nearest neighbors were a very muddy practice field for British tanks (I liked the experience of their thundering by on Heerstrasse with a deafening roar at seven o'clock in the morning, right in the middle of some article from the literary page), a neighborhood grocery with unbelievable prices, and a British cemetery from the Second World War:

"A British Navigator. Died on the 16th of December 1943. Known unto God."

and to the west, just green, dense beech forest for nearly a two-hour walk.

I made a couple of small attempts to get away.

I made a trip to Stockholm to tape a TV program, but it ended by my getting a fever of 104 while sitting in a bar talking with Myrdal and Stolpe about Roman church sculpture.

I made a trip to Vienna and sat in Café Landtmann on Ringstrasse, discussing Byzantine culture with Dr. Urbach, and right there at Café Landtmann I came down with a 104-degree fever and returned home.

Wherever I went, I got a 104-degree fever.

Every time I succeeded in dragging myself back to Scholtzplatz, I got well the moment I went out into the kitchen and had a cup of coffee.

I came to the conclusion that home was at Scholtzplatz.

It was a funny place to call home. I used to get up at seven o'clock, see that the children got breakfast and follow them to the bus which took them along the huge cloverleaves and curves of the expressways into the city in a half hour or so, then sat at my desk straight to three in the afternoon, with breaks only for small, strong cups of a coffee only I can make.

The one thing I really demand from life is to be allowed to write in peace.

On occasion I would venture into the city, to browse in bookstores and meet people.

For the most part I would spend the afternoons on really long walks through Grunewald, through the young green forest all the way to Hundekehlensee.

Tiny green algae filled Hundekehlensee, with its ducks, its plastic milk cartons floating around, its green banks, its fake Renaissance castles built by industrial magnates of the last century.

I have friends at Hundekehlensee.

On the way there you pass over two hills, or rather between two hills, that lie in the middle of the indistinct suburban landscape like two bizarre female breasts. One is more peculiar than the other.

The one to the right is a natural hill, covered by grass and trees and bushes and at the top some kind of Wagnerian Graal castle for an American radar station. The Graal castle has gigantic white domes and is guarded by American soldiers armed to the teeth, with huge beasts for watchdogs.

If you could only be certain it is a radar station and nothing worse! Presumably it keeps track of all of the East European air space from here to Novgorod, but how can you be sure it isn't also listening in to our conversations, reading our thoughts, preparing some terrible catastrophe?

Maybe it's a secret research station dealing with previously unknown magic weapons? Perhaps it does something with our language, with our dreams?

The hill to the left is completely bare, except for the emerald-green grass that covers it at this time of year.

You ponder for a while where you've seen it before, and suddenly you know.

In western Asia, in Asia Minor, there are hills like that.

They contain ruined cities.

An archeologist's wild strawberry patch.

You go down through the strata. First bricks and then stone, and then bricks, and finally remains of primitive pole structures where the dead were buried in rubbish heaps and bones lie scorched in the ashes of some hearth that stopped burning thousands of years ago.

And below the most primitive earth floor, a marble floor with a wonderful mosaic.

And so on.

This one in Grunewald is six hundred and fifty feet high. It's always blowing at the top. Here and there half of an old bathtub is sticking out of the ground, as if the mountain were in the process of giving birth to it. Ever so often your foot gets stuck in something, you pull and struggle, and suddenly you're holding onto a big chunk from a stylish Victorian cast-iron ornament.

It clinks, a couple of blue tiles slide a short way down the slope and come to rest in some nettles.

You never see anyone here, just the trace of some kind of bobsled run, and that is used only in the winter, but a strong and persistent wind is blowing. The first gust reminds me right away of my friend Sigismund

BUT HE IS STILL SLEEPING

and from the top I go off in the direction of Hundekehlensee, always toward Hundekehlensee, visible far off to the northwest like a little reflection of light in the verdure. The road goes through garden lots, more forest, more gardens, more forest, and you never feel really safe until you hear the sound of the freeway to Dreilinden and see the old S-Bahn station, wall-papered with spiderwebs, emerge from the greenery.

That forest always frightens me a little.

There is, how shall I put it,

HUNTING IN THE AIR

a hunting horn under the trees' green crowns, I have the feeling that some bizarre hunting party could at any moment overtake me on their horses—hunters in red coats and the ladies in red dresses, surrounded by hounds, lots of black-spotted, lively Dalmatians, and the ladies' and gentlemen's faces looking a little *strange*, a little deformed, like faces become from having lain a long time in the earth—and join in a chase over the countryside. With yapping hounds at their heels I would be chased until my lungs hurt and I couldn't manage another step, and in some light glade a few years later someone would find my wristwatch, lightly trampled, with a cobwebby pattern on the watch face.

AND WITH THE HANDS AT THREE-THIRTY

and it is time for tea.

It's been afternoon for several months.

And now, ever deeper verdure, ever deeper twilight under the trees, where the number 17 bus makes its way in an aquarium of foliage and filtered afternoon light on its long route between Grunewald and Lichterfelde.

And I sit on a stone bench down on the bank of Wannsee and see a huge, muffled, oppressive thunderstorm towering above the horizon to the north, over the city. The large lake surface in front of me is full of restless sailboats crossing back and forth. Among lilacs in the huge abandoned garden behind me comes a forlorn murmur, and the smell of the flowers reminds me of certain early summer afternoons that could also last for months in Ramnäs during my childhood, and for the first time in years I think about the youngest of my mother's brothers and sisters. Most of them were brothers, my uncles, but the youngest was a sister, Aunt Clara, and I liked her more than all the rest put together, and she was more gifted, more eccentric than all the others.

I really wonder what happened to her.

THE FIRST GUST OF WIND TURNS THE PAGES IN MY BOOK, TURNS THEM

so that it reads itself, the way a Tibetan prayer wheel manages by itself, and I sit completely straight without reading a line and look across the lake to the thunder and lightning building up over the new, hideous steam-generating plant in Lichterfelde.

This morning when I woke up in my room, piled with books and manuscripts and my son's model airplanes of the First World War—he builds model airplanes of the First World War so fast that no one knows what to do with them except stick them in my room, and I often wake up with the remaining parts of a crashed Handley Page 0/4000 under my back. This morning when I woke up and looked up to the ceiling, where a Messerschmitt is engaged in a perpetual dogfight with a Bristol, each hanging from its own thread from the light fixture, I realized I had dreamed a strange, completely insane dream.

It is a dream about myself.

It is a dream about the year 1968.

It is a dream about us.
(which us?)

A hunter caught up with his quarry, a rabbit running in such terror that its backlegs seemed incongruously long.

Now the hunter aims, now he shoots, now the rabbit will finally meet its fate.

But then something completely unexpected happens.

Something bigger snares them both.

The whole scene is enclosed in crystal or the sort of clear, polished, plastic block you use to encase flowers and shells.

The wind over the hills brings with it the smell of coal smoke, exhaust fumes, French fries, hot metal. It is the city blowing out from itself over the green beech forest.

And far off, like a white flash: Hundekehlensee.

Now I've got it:

THE SHOWER OF SHOT, CAPTURED IN FLIGHT IN FRONT OF THE HUNTER'S GUN

The Story About Aunt Clara

She wasn't at all like my uncles. My uncles were fairly large, somewhat rugged men, some unattractive, like Uncle Knutte with his bald head and flabby cheeks, others rather handsome, like Uncle Stig with his square-clipped beard and high temples, which almost made him look like a Polish country nobleman.

They had a squareness, a coarseness. They were the kind of men who cause a boat to rock dangerously when they sit down in it. They moved with heavy, determined steps, so that the floor creaked when they walked on it. They spoke thoughtfully and wrinkled their foreheads deeply, and when you asked them about something, there was always a pause before they came out with an answer.

Aunt Clara, who was the youngest of my mother's brothers and sisters, was of an entirely different constitution.

She was small, dark, lively, with large eyes—much too large, someone said.

Her somewhat wiry, dark-brown hair fell down far below her shoulders. Her eyes could be a little red-rimmed, especially in the early mornings, and when they looked at you over the breakfast table, they had a strange nobility: you didn't feel as *refined* as she.

She was a rather small woman who moved through the world with dancing steps and spoke in a dark, very pretty contralto.

When she came to visit us in the summer she used to wear a red polka dot dress that left her pretty shoulders bare. She didn't tan. She was always just a little bit pale.

She spoke quickly and a great deal, and her voice was so beautiful that as a boy I almost never managed to remember what she actually said because when she spoke, it sounded like music.

Certain of Béla Bartók's string quartets even today can send a shiver down my spine, they remind me so strongly of Aunt Clara's purringly soft contralto when she was sitting on the steps in Ramnäs in the morning sun and drinking her coffee.

It was self-evident that Aunt Clara was finer than we, and it was always a great honor when she came to visit. When she arrived at the station on the three o'clock bus, she was as a matter of course picked up by taxi. Papa wore something resembling a summer suit when she came, beer was out of the question, and we made sure she always had a glass and a pitcher of water by her bedside, not because she needed it but because she was so refined.

I loved her very much. One time when she turned to me with her big, blue, critical eyes and looked at me and said, "Lars, won't you show me how far you've got with the boat?"—it tickled me all the way down to my toes in unconcealed joy. It was an acknowledgment that I existed, that in some distant world we were equals, which made the sun shine a little stronger for me the whole day.

I always tried to get so close to her that I could smell the aroma from her small, white upper arms. Even this was different, in some way finer than any other person's smell.

I was in prepuberty, a little slow, a little dumb, and full of anxiety, which found expression in my trying to build myself a plywood boat all summer long. These boats were thrown together and clumsy—on the one hand you couldn't come by any whole sheets of plywood, and on the other I was quite simply so frightfully stupid—and they always sank when they were launched, to the accompaniment of my father's terrible laughter.

Then began a great deal of caulking and fussing with various tars and pitches and glue and God knows what. And it was always the same misery. If I succeeded in caulking them so that they were watertight for three minutes, then the whole bottom of the boat would suddenly fall out instead.

Aunt Clara was the only one who didn't laugh. She used to sit in a beach chair down at the shore, with a large white sunhat over her brown hair, smelling of various suntan lotions, and sometimes she would look up over the top of her *Femina* and observe me with her big, mysterious eyes, as I with my bare boys' shoulders struggled and toiled with plane and hammer and saw over my intractable and cursed pieces of plywood.

93

It felt strange. And nice. And confusing.

Aunt Clara had a secret. It was in her smell, in her voice, it was always there as a question in her large eyes.

There was a ring of caution around her. People never spoke about her when by chance she was in some other room.

People always spoke about my uncles. They said:

"He hasn't been drinking again?"

or

"Is he inventing things again? He's *not* going to take the pump apart another time? I'm going crazy!"

When Aunt Clara went out for a moment to get her suntan lotion or cigarettes (she smoked all the time, and her small narrow fingertips were yellow from nicotine, and Mama thought it was awful for a lady to smoke, but she never said anything about it), there was just a polite silence.

You didn't *make comments* about her.

And occasionally there were telephone calls. Very often for that matter.

Right across the road lived a former sawmill foreman named Isaksson, a large, heavy man with melancholy eyes, arms that were too long, and a funny stooped gait.

He had periodically been in charge of the whole mill, but as he himself said, he wasn't really "suited" to the work, and of his own free will he had retired to live on his beekeeping, selling decorative jars with the blue- and yellow-guarantee of the Royal Society of Swedish Beekeepers around the middle.

You couldn't get potatoes as good as his.

Even after his time as sawmill foreman he had kept his telephone. It sat very neatly on a little crocheted cloth in his sitting room, on a separate table of brown mahogany that must have originally been intended to hold a flowerpot. God knows what he used it for. We would ask to use the telephone on rare occasions when there was something especially important and urgent that had to be taken care of. A constant nuisance, for example, were those demonic toothaches in my decaying babyteeth, which I used to get one or two times every summer, and then we had to call the dentist in Västerås and make an appointment. With crying and gritting my teeth, misery of miseries on the bus in, a bag of candy as consolation and perhaps a book, and worse on the bus back when it hurt even more and I had to sit there and look normal because I was old enough that it wasn't proper to sit there and whine.

When Aunt Clara was with us the telephone rang every other day. The former sawmill foreman Isaksson came with his long hanging arms and a certain inexpressibly sad look in his face and said:

"It's the telephone for the young lady again."

And she brightened up and danced away up Isaksson's garden path.

She talked as long as she wanted to. Aunt Clara had no unusually great respect for telephones. She herself was a switchboard operator, I forgot to mention that. And not at any old place.

She was a switchboard operator at Sveriges Riksbank, where her deep contralto was really perfect. The deep-red gold in her voice when she answered, unvaryingly impersonal, "Sveriges Riksbank," reflection of the mysterious and somewhat frightening gold that lay stored there in endless quantities in their subterranean chambers and which was the guarantee for Sweden's Monetary Value and Third Defense Loan and the state-issued Government Bonds for 1945.

Europe lay in wreckage. Marshal Zhukov's and marshal Montgomery's armies had victoriously ground their way from the Caucasus to the S-Bahn station at Bornholmerstrasse, from Monte Cassino to Akazienstrasse; the residents of Berlin walked around listlessly and cleaned up their piles of stone and ate their potato soup; the Marshall Plan was already being developed in Washington. Sweden's Per Albin Hansson was toying with the idea of continuing to govern jointly with the nonsocialist parties, since there were now no real problems between parties any more in the postwar period; our liberated neighbors had experienced their summer of joy; and over his large, Spartanly simple mahogany desk in the Kremlin, Generalissimo Joseph Stalin had lit the day's eighth short, broad Dunhill pipe, filled with fine Caucasian tobacco, and with short stubby fingers turned the pages in a report from the Third White Russian Front concerning difficulties with railroad cars and locomotives.

Over the Pacific Ocean kamikaze pilots were still buzzing, poor souls, in their white scarves and knew that no one would ever dare speak about them with anything but respect as long as the world lasts, for life is so terrible that nothing else instills such respect as to say the hell with everything, and the atom bombs that were to fall over Hiroshima and Nagasaki already existed as parts in factories, and history was on the whole too large for people.

"What's The Russian going to do now," said old Lindvall, who was watering his lilacs on the road down to Kyrkbyn.

He was always talking about "The Russian" and "The German," as if each were only a single person, one with a black beard and the other with a black moustache, an evil sneer, and a Prussian lieutenant's monocle in his eye.

People were dumbfounded by everything the world could think of for the radio to report and gradually began to say the hell with everything. They grew cabbage and tended their currant bushes instead.

August 1945. I don't think the turnips and currants and rhubarb have ever done as well in Västmanland as that year. The house-painter Nisse Eklund in Seglingsberg (as a matter of fact he was the one who taught me to read science-fiction novels, he had bundles of *Adventure* magazine in his attic) said it had to have something to do with the war, a subtle biological balance that had been upset and had to be re-established and, who knows, he might have been right.

At the beginning of August, before the atom bombs had fallen, Aunt Clara came on her last summer visit to Västmanland. We didn't know then, of course, that it would be the last.

She was a little frantic. She had a few more telephone conversations than usual, and they lasted a little longer than usual.

Then we began to discover that there was something strange going on.

She came back so red with tears after some of these conversations that even the former sawmill foreman Isaksson began to lend her his flowered handkerchiefs. And he was not at all a sensitive person.

She came back, small, her whole body shaking with rage and sorrow, struck her fist on the table, rushed to her room and threw herself on the couch, or tore down to the dock and sat there, small and cowering, and looked out over the setting sun for hours, so that we really didn't know what to do with her.

It was clear that something had gone wrong.

Aunt Clara had a dark secret. The family never really knew whether it should treat it as a thing to be proud of or to be ashamed of.

Good God, after all these years I hardly remember anymore how things were, that's what happens when you keep a secret too long! As August Strindberg says, you shouldn't have any secrets! And not other people either.

As I said, she was a switchboard operator at Sveriges Riksbank, and at such a remarkable place, so far above the everyday world, she couldn't avoid coming into contact with the sort of people who were so notable and so highly placed that for us they were only topics to be discussed in the daily news.

One of those really highly placed people must have cast his eyes on Aunt Clara.

The whole thing was, as I have said, very mysterious, very mystical, and we only whispered about it.

Perhaps it was the chairman of the bank's Board of Directors? Or the president of the Lower Judicial Review? I know that I knew it then, but on my life I can't recall it now.

I only remember that it was a person who at any moment could be expected to become a minister in the new government, which could be formed at any time, when the coalition government left office—a very highly placed person indeed.

So Aunt Clara had a sure shot at becoming the wife of a government minister.

There were only a few formal details lacking. For example, this really highly placed person had to make up his mind finally to get a divorce, and that was clearly not an easy matter. In the highest circles, you have to do it at the right moment, so as not to disturb your career.

To get a divorce just when a new government is going to be formed, and when you yourself are projected to succeed Finance Minister Wigforss or Welfare Minister Möller, is not socially acceptable. Anyone can understand that.

This is certainly why Aunt Clara was unhappy.

In the neighborhood of Ramnäs at that time there was a very bizarre old ragman. God only knows what his name actually was, but I think that it was for fun that everyone first began to call him Gottwold.

I saw Gottwold as being rather old then, in his seventies or so, but it is possible that he was a bit younger.

He was a rather strong man, completely blind. Over his sightless eyes he wore a pair of ancient, blue-green eyeglasses with steel rims, from his jaw hung an extremely long gray-black beard, sticky with the remains of his breakfast, and chewing tobacco ran from the corner of his mouth and God only knows what else. I think it was an explosion that had blinded him—some time in his youth he had worked at the foundryworks in Ramnäs.

Now he went around along the roads, blind and groping his way, with a steady jet of saliva mixed with tobacco streaming from his beard. Behind him Gottwold always pulled a little wagon, which looked like a tiny haycart with all his stuff: scrap iron that he collected and sold again, old empty bottles, bicycle spokes, discarded thermoses, his raincoat, so full of holes and rips, an umbrella, and a very large package, wrapped in waterproof cloth, that no one ever got a look at.

Gottwold was kind to children. When he came along the road, smiling in his strange way and humming and whimpering to himself, the wagon rattling after him in the gravel as he groped with his white cane for the grassy median in the road (he avoided the big highways), the children came running in throngs. But no one really came up with the idea of annoying him.

We would get to sit in his wagon and plow through all the strange objects which were there, everything but that mysterious package in the waterproof cloth, and we got to pull his beard and long bristly white hair and look at an old pewter watch with odd figures (there was a series of animals instead of hours on the watch face: a crayfish, a bull, a curious man who was carrying water, an ox with bent horns) that he pulled out from under his old brown wool sweater with the white darning.

And the dolls. One of the wares he sold at the farms was a sort of merry little ragdoll, small girl-dolls he had sewn together out of sackcloth, old stockings, and rags into strangely illusory, tiny female creatures.

They would always sit farthest back in the little haycart and pathetically swing their arms over the side when he pulled it on through the gravel.

He sold them to the small children at the farms where he would get a splash of coffee in the kitchen, if people weren't too frightened of his smell, which rose like a saint's halo around him.

His nose was coarse, with a powerful hook, almost a hump, in the middle, but his upper lip was surprisingly sensitive.

When you saw him it was easy to think: this is the demolished basement of something else, of another sort of person than he became.

Without that explosion, perhaps he would have become something remarkable.

You could also say that he was rather remarkable the way he was.

My mother would always invite him for cookies and juice on the steps when he came by with his cart once or twice every summer. And he used to take all of our empty bottles with him.

The summer didn't feel quite complete until he had been there.

That year, 1945, a long time passed before he came, all the way to the middle of August.

It was exactly the same day that Aunt Clara received her last call from the future government minister.

It was catastrophic and lasted a very long time. I think she talked on the telephone so long that the former sawmill foreman Isaksson managed to empty and clearn four beehives before it was over, and it ended quite dreadfully, because Aunt Clara hung up the receiver with such a bang that the telephone's metal hooks barely withstood the strain, and she rushed out, red with anger and tears.

The future government minister, you see, had finally decided to say the hell with the political risks and allow his emotions to claim their due and get married, but not to Aunt Clara.

It was one of those lightly overcast, warm summer days when it has rained all night and the sun is just trying to break out of the cloud cover. The currants hung thickly on the bushes in Isaksson's garden patch. A few crows were hopping hesitantly around the imaginatively constructed scarecrows.

A train passed by at the railroad tracks, an endless line of empty, rattling ore cars, and Aunt Clara was wondering through her tears where in God's name so many cars could be going.

A chicken hawk was hovering and cruising in the wind above the big forest on the other side of the lake. A tree was quivering in a barely noticeable breeze and shook a few heavy raindrops over Aunt Clara's round, narrow, very feminine shoulders.

Her hands in front of her face, she walked around crying, all alone in the world, her expression blank, despairing and seen by everyone.

The blind vagabond Gottwold had meanwhile managed to pull his wagon into our yard and park it neatly inside the fence. He was sitting on our veranda drinking coffee so that it trickled into his beard and eating my mother's best napoleons. His large, blue blindman's glasses shined emptily out into space, and he was engaged in a very monosyllabic conversation with my mother about the weather and wind and forks in the road and the forest clearings.

My mother, small and round and friendly in her white print dress with blue dots on it, was carrying on a monologue that Gottwold occasionally interrupted with

"Yeah, that's right, always"

and this

"Yeah, that's right, always"

which came with such a terrible monotony that you could certainly have reasons for doubting he cared at all about what he was saying.

And that was really pretty silly of him, since my mother's monologues can actually be extremely entertaining if you listen closely to what she is saying.

He had so clumsily put one shoe against the electric heater on the veranda that it smelled strongly of burned leather, but it didn't seem as though he had noticed anything at all.

I, who was standing expectantly close by, listening to the

monotone conversation, and occasionally trying to move sideways to get a peek under those blue eyeglasses to see what it looked like behind them

(were the eyes still there?)

discovered it first, though it took me quite a while before I was able to explain to him what was actually happening.

He pulled back his shoe, which was quite badly burned, with a detached air, as though it hardly belonged to him.

At that moment, Aunt Clara came in through the door, small and trembling and completely white in the face.

Outside, the crows were making noise in the flowerbed.

Gottwold looked up immediately—yes, he really *looked up* and for a moment set his blank, blue-green eyeglass lenses on Aunt Clara.

He wasn't entirely unlike some big, clumsy animal that has suddenly picked up a scent. He sniffed with his heavy head in various directions.

And it was unbelievable. Aunt Clara fell forward toward him, almost as if the lousy, blind vagabond had been her father, buried her weeping head somewhere inside his awful coat, disappeared with her soft, trembling shoulders somewhere inside his long beard.

Amazed and unable to believe our own eyes, we stood there and watched Gottwold's large, slightly purple hand brush over her small narrow head with its fine brown hair, just brush over it paternally, again and again, just brush . . .

Both Mama and I understood that it was something wonderful, something terrible and wonderful we were witnessing, and didn't let a word pass our lips.

It was in the middle of August. Late in the afternoon. Yes, if I remember correctly, just then the sun broke out and dried up after the rain.

Aunt Clara went with Gottwold the same afternoon. She left

most of her luggage behind, because there wasn't a lot of room in Gottwold's cart.

There wasn't much mama and I could do. We stood by the fence, quite moved, both of us watching them disappear around the bend in the road, hand in hand. The cart rattled and jerked in the loose gravel at the curve.

"Don't you at least want to take your toothbrush," shouted Mama, with real desperation in her voice.

"No thanks," Aunt Clara shouted back. "It's not necessary."

I think that was the first time in my life I saw an example of how enormous man's freedom can be, if you begin to believe it, and it taught me a great deal.

If the truth were known, Papa got quite furious when he came home in the evening. He had been in Västerås, to take care of some extremely pressing business.

"For God's sake, you've got to go to Isaksson at once and call the district police," Papa said, purple in the face. He has a tendency to take things seriously, which I unfortunately have inherited from him. (If I had only taken after my mother—I'd have been a much funnier writer.)

Of course, Mama hadn't thought of that, of our calling the district police.

"You have to give him a precise description of them. Both of them," Father said.

"But . . ."

"No buts. Anything could happen."

"But no crime has been committed," Mama said calmly.

It took him almost an hour of total metaphysical brooding before he understood that neither Gottwold nor Aunt Clara had done anything that could justify calling the police out with bloodhounds and radio vehicles. For love between adults of clearly opposite sexes the law had not placed any limits on, even in the forties.

And of course it had been wise not to.

They had been seen in Surahammar. Some months later rumors surfaced that both had spent the night in the barn in Söderbärke. They became a legend the whole district talked about. They turned up everywhere, extremely happy, very much in love. She led the blindman through the autumn rain, along the muddy roads, under old railroad viaducts, and into barns where they spent their nights. Everywhere they were received with a singular veneration, the kind of deep veneration that only total, complete love can instill in people. They created, you could say without really exaggerating, a light over the entire autumn landscape.

Unfortunately, Aunt Clara's lungs weren't strong enough. She couldn't take sleeping under railroad viaducts and in damp winter barns. She fell ill with pneumonia during the March thaw and died in the living room of a kind farmer in Haraker. Gottwold sat with her right to the end, he caught her last look in his blue, unfathomable eyeglasses.

I think she died completely happy.

And they became a legend that even today people tell in front of their fireplaces in Västmanland, late on winter evenings, after the last TV program has ended.

The story of Clara and Gottwold. Just think, she was my aunt—Clara!

Gottwold survived her by several decades. He died in the infirmary of Nibble retirement home in Hallstahammar (Hallstahammar was the only community that could be prevailed upon to take care of him, because he had a nearly illegible paper that supposedly proved he belonged to Berg parish, which nowadays is a part of the greater municipality of Hallstahammar) the same day that President Kennedy was murdered. My Grandmother Tekla, who eventually would celebrate her hundredth birthday in the same retirement home a decade later, knew him very well and would occasionally give him a food parcel when he was sitting and slobbering in the dayroom of the infirmary.

"Gottwold is so kind and nice. You know, he's a remarkable

104

man, a remarkable young man," Grandmother Tekla used to say, looking at me with her very old, wise eyes, which had seen daylight since the days of the Paris Commune and which nothing could astonish anymore.

I think Tekla knew a little something of his role in the family's history, because she would screw her eyes up a bit.

"Such a fine young man, and dead so early," she said on the telephone the morning President Kennedy was murdered, sounding quite moved.

"President Kennedy?"

"I beg your pardon?"

"The American president?"

"What about him?"

"I thought you were speaking about him?"

"I'm speaking about Gottwold the Blindman. He's dead."

And the package in the waterproof cloth? The one so carefully wrapped? Mrs. Bergkloo, the manager of the retirement home, opened all of his possessions. The package turned out to contain two huge manuscripts, written on paper of extremely varying quality and size. They were both about one thousand pages long, evidently amounting to two novels.

Through a fortunate occurrence on the same day that she read through them and was thinking of carrying them down to the retirement home's incinerator, Mrs. Bergkloo was visited by a young man from Västerås, sent by the provincial antiquarian as a part of that year's inventory of the archives in Västmanland.

Mrs. Bergkloo got it into her head that Gottwold's two manuscripts might perhaps be something for him, and he hestitantly took them along in his Volkswagen when he left.

The two manuscripts of Gottwold the Blindman are kept in the Provincial Archives in Västerås under the classification "GHG (Hallstahammar and environs, folklore) 23467992 A" and "23467992 B," respectively.

I have read both huge manuscripts—with difficulty, because

some of the paper is old and creased bag paper. And the traces of saliva and snuff have left their mark.

There are two novels, both extremely remarkable.

One deals with the occupation and the final conquest of a city.

All very lively, colorful, with an illusory richness of fantasy. A masterpiece.

The other one, a sort of sequel, and probably written, at least up to the last sections, during the happy autumn and winter with Clara, deals with one of the heroes of the occupation who, in the course of long sea voyage home, is steadily drawn into new adventures and entanglements. Also a masterpiece. Very lively, with remarkable allegorical and philosophical values.

Finally, the hero reaches his home tract, which he has given up all hope of ever seeing again.

His wife's house is occupied by suitors. He overcomes them all through cunning and great strength. He and his wife are united at last.

Her name is Clara.

I don't think Aunt Clara ever had a clue that these novels existed.

Another World

A springlike haze lay over Berlin those days. Heavy, sticky chestnut branches swept over the roofs of the doubledecker buses. The air was damp and heavy with odors. There was unrest in the air.

The Mampestube Café on Kurfürstendamm put out their outdoor tables and chairs. Cute girls in blue jeans began to appear on the streets.

An old hack of a horse fell down dead in the middle of the traffic at Tempelhofer Damm. A sparrow was sitting on its head when the police arrived to see what could be done with the cadaver.

In the quiet, friendly Turkish quarters in Kreuzberg the fruit and vegetable merchants were beginning to move their tables out onto the streets, so that they soon looked like Oriental bazaars, and tightly veiled women thronged in front of the counters and squeezed the fruits with practiced expressions of Anatolian farmers' wives.

Horsemen were riding through Grunewald. Noiselessly, the soft, mossy field caught the horses' hooves.

In the subway, between Ernst Reuther-Platz and Heidelberger Platz, a huge construction project was underway that spring.

What could be seen of it when you passed by on the train was the tunnel abruptly widening into a huge vault where a chaos of enormous girders was illuminated by sudden flashes of fire. Yugoslav and Turkish workers climbed around in this bewildering space without clear dimensions, heavy crane cars swung the huge beams into place, and an awful roar of drills, pumps, and bulldozers reverberated under the great vaults, which smelled strongly of hot metal and newly poured concrete. "A raw smell, almost like war or natural catastrophes," thought the painter G. when the subway train, the first that morning, suddenly stopped at this station.

107

Belo, Uriel, and Azaar, with mysteriously fresh-shaved, rested faces, rose up cheerfully as though ready to get out of the train.

It was they who had suggested to her that their journey should begin on the subway, and she couldn't help laughing one of her rare, open, clean laughs at the whole suggestion, since to some extent it fit in with the ideas she had formed about the whole expedition.

And now the train stopped here, of all conceivable places. The din from the pneumatic machines outside all but caused the subway train's windowpanes to vibrate.

"Dear friend," said Belo, chivalrously offering her his arm while Uriel pulled out her suitcase from under the seat (she had been somewhat uncertain about what might be necessary on such a trip: toothbrush, wool sweater, after some hesitation a small torchon-paper sketchpad and some watercolors, and then one other thing that she had been hesitant about for a long time), "we have to change here!"

"But there isn't a stop here," said the painter G., who didn't care very much for noise and thought the place quite unpleasant on the whole.

"This is an extra train," said Belo.

And as a matter of fact, the doors opened. They climbed out (they were obviously the only passengers in the whole car) onto what was not a platform but simply a rather narrow gangway or bridge resting on steel scaffolding. The din was earsplitting, and through the openings in the planks she could see far below, at least one hundred and fifty feet beneath them, amid infernal noise and the light of strong searchlights, a dredge digging in the fine yellow postdiluvial sand of Berlin.

"Careful, it can be slippery," shouted Belo into her ear. "It's just a little further."

They met workers in yellow safety helmets, engineers with sliderules behind their ears, except no one seemed to notice them in the least. The painter G. thought it was odd, but she had experienced too many strange things during the previous night and morning to be able to be surprised any longer.

"Wouldn't it have been more comfortable to leave from Tempelhof," she shouted back into Belo's ear.

"You can't book a flight this early in the morning, and besides," Belo shouted back, "it's no fun to stand there and be shoved at the doors by fat old ladies." He appeared to be in an excellent humor.

They must have gone at least a hundred feet along the narrow gangway, which had only a protective bar on one side, and instinctively the painter G. turned toward it when they met some workers. "Good God, how can people stand to work in such a disgusting environment," she thought and cast a frightened glance at the small, shortlegged, sturdy Turks with their mustaches and yellow oilskin gear who they were steadily running into or who, carrying huge monkey wrenches, were running into them.

At the end of the gangway there was a steel structure, and in front of it what appeared to be a safety exit, covered with chickenwire. Belo pushed on a yellow button mounted on the doorframe. Everyone waited. Uriel, who had clearly got tired of carrying her suitcase, had put it down between his legs.

She wondered what in all her born days they were waiting for. The earsplitting racket and blue flames of the welding torches were giving her a headache. It was absolutely impossible to make yourself heard, so she had to content herself with casting uneasy and inquisitive glances at her three companions. They all looked very calm, very energetic, like three young attachés on the way to a meeting, she thought to herself. In these surroundings, they seemed more ordinary than up on the earth's surface.

Suddenly something moved in front of her, and she understood that what they had been standing and waiting for was quite simply an elevator, a crude hoist with grating for doors, protected by plain chickenwire, the kind of thing used to carry workers and materials to lower levels.

The safety net in front of them slid up on its wires, and they stepped in.

We leave them there for a moment.

It occurs to me that I am presently describing a descent into Hell, but not only that, but even in a rather benevolent fellow-traveler's spirit.

From my window where I am writing, it is a very beautiful August morning in Väster Våla. The dew is just leaving the grass, and I have spent the whole hour between six and seven driving Per Brusling's damned bulls out of my vegetable patch, alternating between wild yelling and paternal, admonishing blows on the back with my walking stick. Through the window I see the white church in Väster Våla appear between the trees. And it occurs to me that my friend the curate wouldn't really approve of what I am working on. And the question is whether or not the Bishop of Västerås ought to be brought into the matter. As the Swedish proverb says, he who starts with a pin ends with a silver goblet, and anyway we know how it went for witch trials in Mora. Can we have a *fellow traveler* in the diocese?

You can ask yourself whether or not the bulls were a warning: is it completely *normal* that thirty black bulls suddenly station themselves in a private person's vegetable patch and tramp around, and only in his—not in Jansson's, the crafts instructor, nor in Sundelin's, the contractor, only in mine?

The only thing missing now is for Brusling to call up and say that he has thirty bulls too many!

In my youth, when I was strongly influenced by the ideas of the Enlightenment (I still am for that matter, since there have hardly been any better ideas since then), I saw it as my task to demonstrate the irrationality of the religious imagination.

Hell? Ha! Where is it, anyway? Under the earth? But every schoolchild knows that under the earth there is only magma and, furthest in, a core of iron! Or somewhere else? Where then? In a galaxy, in the constellation Swan? So you, sir, claim, in complete seriousness, that there are, in the Swan, little men with horns and fire pokers who boil souls in sulfur and monsters with armored penises who rape old massage-parlor managers? What's the number of the ambulance again? Yes, it's bad. It's probably best to take along a doctor with a syringe and straitjacket. Quite right. Exactly. Too bad.

And as regards an omnipotent and benevolent God, I have my objections. If I were omnipotent and benevolent, I wouldn't at all claim that everything ought to be perfect. I couldn't possibly resist the temptation of bringing about a wildly itching eczema on some literary critic and putting a bull's head on Franco and a gnome's nose on Nixon, and some of my actions in this guise would surely look more or less like a relapse into the Greek gods' self-indulgent practices.

But I think I would be able to guarantee that if I were omnipotent and benevolent, we wouldn't have had the battles of Sombreil and Verdun, Auschwitz and Hiroshima, nor the suppression of the Sepoy Rebellion and child labor in the English mines in the 1860s.

I could make the list a bit longer, if you want, you old masturbating galaxy carpenter, but I think you know it yourself!

That's right, I said masturbating galaxy carpenter, and I mean it. And now don't go and send a thunderbolt and transform me into an obituary notice in *Expressen*. That would certainly be very impressive, very stylish, and undoubtedly an argument for Pastor Stanley Sjöberg if three minutes from now I'm found as a pile of whimpering ash slouched over my melted typewriter, but don't imagine that that is any real argument.

You don't argue by force, least of all if you are omnipotent and benevolent.

"How's this: higher plan?"

"Did you really say, higher plan?"

"Yes, indeed." *Higher plan*, did you really say that? Not even the minister of finance would venture into such misguided casuistry.

"Tell it like it is. You have no damned idea where you're going, you're falling blindly into time's endless wellhole like all of us, and the distant galaxies are falling with you. You're a blind animal beyond the distant radio horizon of the universe, more intelligent than we, that's true, since you created us, but far from conscious of who you are, engrossed in the millennium-slow thumping of your huge, dark heart, endlessly listening to the cascade of quasars that roar in your own interior, surprised as a young mother at the first sporadic spasms of consciousness in your enormous womb.

Of course you're a young mother! I know who you are, a mentally retarded young girl whom someone has got pregnant and who is sitting in the dayroom of a mental ward, despised by everyone in your unsightly institutional dress, which stretches over your large shapeless stomach, and uncomprehending, with huge empty eyes, you feel the unborn life kicking inside you. Only that way can I love you.

It's not hard to make an assault on the gods. But one point is easily missed: the historical.

In my youth, in the seminar of the famous atheist, Professor Hedenius, I felt strongly that it was my duty to convert young theology students to atheism.

If I had succeeded, a bunch of agreeable men who wouldn't harm a fly would today be woefully keeping records at the Unemployment Office, at a minimum subsistence level, instead of sitting in pleasant country houses, with sheep and chickens and nice private libraries, and a little work tossing out a few respectable lines from Mark 5:2 on Friday afternoons.

If I had been consistent, I ought to have gone to Mecca, too, at the end of Ramadan, to convert young Moslems to Professor Hedenius' views.

Why don't I do that? For fear of the Saudi Arabian prisons and the lack of travel grants for such expeditions, I guess.

But there is another reason.

Let us assume that Mohammed at the time of his flight from Mecca to Medina was a hysterical sheik, epileptic, repetitive, quarrelsome, self-centered, rolling around in convulsive revelations. An unbearable person who quite correctly wasn't allowed to stay in Mecca.

There is quite a lot to say for such a theory.

For my historical intuition Jesus is a Baader-Meinhof type: a desperate radical of the Essene sect, he can't stay in Qumran, goes to Jerusalem and jeopardizes the meager Occupation existence of the entire Jewish people by starting a Temple rebellion right in the middle of Passover, proclaims himself the king of the Jews, and is sacrificed for the sake of social tranquility by influential political circles who see that things will go completely to hell if such an unexpected insurrection were to break out. In that way, the inevitable disintegration is drawn out to the year 66, and though for us it might appear as an insignificant gain, the same argument can be used very well against the French Communist Party in 1968.

Jesus is a remarkable example of what is usually meant by "bourgeois impatience" and "adventurous anarchism."

To return to Mohammed. Let us assume that he was an epileptic sheik who rolls around in frothing convulsions and chases women with a stick among the tents.

One and a half thousand years later, he is not that. For all that time, millions of people have devoted to him their love, their lives, their breath, their best ideas, their highest aspirations, their most refined masterpieces.

For millions of people, he is the meaning of history, the content of their lives. So much love, so much goodwill is not found in vain.

Kiss enough times the simple icon with a black olive tree painted on its stem (I am thinking here of a poem by Gunnar Ekelöf), and it becomes holy. Your hand in your pocket, squeeze often enough the black stone you once got from a young witch in Ohrid, and it begins to live.

113

It is man who is a godmaker. It is history that creates gods, and their power comes from all the love we have given them.

Could the simple houses of prayer with red-stained wood in northern Västmanland ever have come into existence if they hadn't expressed something? Could the innermost longings of a thousand thin tenant farmers' wives, blue from the cold, have been meaningless and absolutely without force?

You can't make me believe that.

The professor is wrong. Both Heaven and Hell exist because history exists and to try to remove them in a couple of neatly constructed broadcast lectures is less clever than when Thor tries to pick up the World Serpent because he thinks it is an old barnyard cat.

The young mentally retarded young girl with the empty eyes sits in the dayroom just as quiet as before. There is life under her big stomach.

How gladly I would put my hand on it and feel!

"It's falling very rapidly. If you're the least bit prone to dizziness, I'd advise you to hold onto my hand."

It was Belo who was talking. The painter G. was so confused by the whole situation that she took his advice. The burning hot hand spread a peculiar warmth over her whole body.

The racket and air in the shaft did not agree with her.

"Good God, just let it go quickly," she thought with the same panicky feeling you get when an airplane motor is put on full throttle and you see there is no turning back any longer: the takeoff has to succeed or else you'll be killed.

Not without a certain gratitude, she squeezed the offered hand. It was very hot, almost like a very hot shower on the verge of scalding you, and she had a strange feeling that it was getting hotter every moment.

"Good God, just let it go quickly," she thought again.

But at first the elevator went as slowly as any construction hoist. They passed through the floor levels of the huge subway project. Amazed workers with wheelbarrows and steel girders on small wagons stopped and waited for the elevator now and then. Patiently they watched it move by. When they passed below the bottom floor, the Turkish workers were startled. They seemed to shout something after them, but she couldn't make out what they said in the racket from the rock-drills.

Now the elevator picked up speed, accelerating tremendously in a few seconds, and the painter G. experienced a feeling not unlike the one the astronauts must feel when their huge rockets lift off from Cape Canaveral, only with the difference that here things were without a doubt headed downward instead.

But what is upward and what is downward? Is the constellation Swan above or below us?

When the awful feeling in her diaphragm has eased a bit, her first thought was that it was time rather than space she was traveling through. Transparent, empty time in all directions.

Not only the time that has been but also the time that could have been—all possible times.

"We are now in what we call the historyless state," said Belo in a low cultivated voice and let go of her hand.

It occurred to her that there was no longer any racket. A deep silence prevailed around them. Outside the elevator nothing was visible, not a darkness, not a blue sky, but literally nothing.

It was a remarkable experience, and it struck her that if she survived, she ought to try to paint it.

"Here are all the events that have not been realized," said Belo with the tone of a polite tourist guide, leaning close to her ear. "Here Hannibal lost the battle at Cannae. Europe is full of pagodas with small crystal-clear brass bells. The Great Mother of the Gods, Cybele, is worshiped in all of Europe's capitals, dragon-adorned balloons hover over the forests, and in Sweden a Danish dialect of a Semitic language that never had the opportunity to develop is spoken.

"Here Thomas Münzer won the peasants' rebellion in Thuringia, the social revolutions of Europe were carried out before 1600, and in a mature, liberated, rather dull world, it is not the arts that

115

flourish but independence, goodwill, mutual and reciprocal altruism.

"In this Europe, there are no big cities, no industries, no super highways, no Turkish guest workers, but linen mills, zeppelins, sprawling green valleys full of prosperous villages, universities directed toward practical knowledge."

"I don't see anything," the painter G. said, a little disappointed.

"No, of course you can't see anything," Belo said in a voice that, with infinite discretion but full clarity, let her know that she had said something dumb. "Here is a world where the will of the people was victorious in 1848, a problematic, much more troublesome world, yet a *necessary* world, more unlike the contingent world where you live than you could ever imagine. And here is Moslem Europe. Saragossa is the great city, London and Paris are market towns. Prosperity and justice prevail under the scepter of wise caliphs. Public executions take place in the square, but only for the unjust. Mathematics and philosophy—in short, the abstract sciences—flourish. No one has heard of Caravaggio and van Eyck, Cranach and Botticelli, and blue tile covers all public buildings.

"Ugh," the painter G. let escape.

"Strange, yes, but not much worse, not more contingent than the era you yourself live in."

"How long are we going to stay in the historyless state?" There was something in the nothingness outside of the elevator's metal structure that made her uneasy. She had expected some kind of an answer, from "ten seconds more" to "forever," but Belo just looked at his dark modern wristwatch (the most expensive kind, on which electronic digits lit up and changed against a pitch black watch face) and said very politely and exactly:

"Twenty-three minutes more."

But twenty-three minutes also seemed long to her.

She must have been more frightened than she dared to admit to herself, for she suddenly became conscious of her own hand, normally a sensitive and vital painter's hand, convulsively closed around a bar in the elevator and clenched so hard it was completely white.

She no longer felt the least desire to speak with her companions. The sympathy, or let us say the benevolent interest, that Belo especially had evoked in her during the past day was virtually blown away.

Her companions seemed for some reason to be concentrated and tense as well. You could almost get the impression that the merry traveler's mood they had been in for several days was dissipating and that they were trying to resume, as it were, their official or professional roles.

Belo was still very handsome where he stood by himself in a corner of the elevator, with one knee nonchalantly drawn up so that the sole of his elegant Italian shoe was propped up against the wall. But wasn't there under that beautiful mask another feature which was becoming more evident with every passing minute? Something ancient, something of a giant tortoise's centuries of experience and weariness and the endlessly slow beating of its heart?

She hadn't got any further in her thoughts when the elevator suddenly began to vibrate violently. For a panic-filled moment she thought that something really dangerous was happening, and then she realized that the elevator was simply braking.

It must have been maintaining a much higher speed than you would expect, for the braking, which lasted at least ten minutes, was such a turbulent and altogether dizzying episode that even Belo looked a bit pale.

Suddenly the shaking stopped and the elevator sank gently down toward the landing floor. "The last stop," thought the painter G.

Outside, she saw only a weakly illuminated, rather long corridor, and at the end of it a very bright light, not unlike the sunlight in Italy on a high summer day.

Belo courteously opened the door.

With quick steps she walked through the corridor, ready for anything. The walls seemed fashioned out of a very coarse, extremely ancient stone that could hardly be anything other than black basalt.

"Good God," she thought. "Let it go quickly, whatever it is." And at the same instant, the thought struck her:

"I won't even be able to die."

She heard her companion's steady steps behind her in the half-darkness of the corridor. The walls seemed completely dry. Clearly, Uriel was still carrying her suitcase. He smiled encouragingly at her when she turned for an instant to see if it was there.

Toward the end of the corridor, there was a tangible change in the air. She could have sworn it was outdoor air if that hadn't been so utterly impossible.

She had never been so frightened as at that moment, that she knew. She felt an ancient fear grow within her, fought bravely against panic, closed her eyes, and stepped out of the corridor, out into what must have been a strongly lighted room.

The wind which she felt at that very moment against her forehead carried with it an unmistakable smell of large deciduous forests, of water, of all the smells you associate with a normal Italian summer's day somewhere in the vicinity of Lago Maggiore.

She opened her eyes with a real effort of will.

She had been expecting anything, but not this.

She found herself on a sort of loggia, or portico, that had to be a part of a very ancient palace, or perhaps a large villa.

On the checkered marble floor stood a comfortable marble bench, and on it lay a coat, or perhaps simply a blanket, of a beautiful deep-red fabric, carelessly spread out as if some easy-going and rather lazy person had just recently left the room.

Through the ceiling vault streamed fresh spring air. A landscape with lakes, rising blue-green hills, and far away on the horizon extremely high mountains whose peaks were lost in the blue haze.

It was an enchantingly beautiful picture. A gentle breeze was stirring the large lake that had to be several miles distant, and she saw clearly how the wind made channels in the water.

And on the left side of the lake there were actually houses, small ingenious houses with tile roofs, not many but still a real little village.

A bumblebee buzzed over the loggia with a low, methodical sound.

"Well, what do you think," said Belo, who in complete silence had pulled up behind her and was lightly poking at her elbow.

"It's—it's not at all what I had imagined."

"Oh," said Belo.

"To be honest, it's very beautiful, very peaceful."

"Of course you can't judge everything by what's here," Belo said. "There are also really harsh landscapes, terribly dull and monotonous. But here it's beautiful. Yet, you're right . . . It's really beautiful here."

He sighed just then like a tired corporate director. His lizard eyes were no longer centuries but millennia old.

It struck the painter G., who like most German intellectuals had a childish weakness for somewhat older men, that such an ancient hand as the one which was now touching her elbow she would never feel again.

She shivered a little.

Cautious Return to the Main Theme:
Sincerity Is Tried and Given Up Again

THROUGH WHICH LAYERS OF AIR IS THE SUN NOW PASSING THAT COLOR IT YELLOW?

We leave them there for a good while. To be frank, I don't really know what I am going to do with them. I'm no moralist, but if the relationship between these beings becomes somewhat intensified, I will be up against themes that no one in world literature has succeeded in solving.

The whole purpose in sending the painter G. to Hell was to work in that difficult clause into the contract, the only important stipulation: to be another person for a single day.

That's what I need her for.

If she can't bring it about in some other way than through love, then so be it, but she must get the stipulation approved.

Poor girl! What will happen to her? Will she ever be able to experience an earthly man after that?

Ah, what idle chatter! That's how the gossip press earns its money. What else do the suburban ladies of Tensta and Farsta buy it for? The only difference is that I who am paid by the Authors' Fund can make it a bit clearer:

The dream about the love of a demon.

I damn well ought to be able to make something really good out of it!

HIS COAL-BLACK HAND RESTING ON THE LEFT CUP OF HER ALMOST COMPLETELY RIPPED-OFF BRASSIERE WAS NOW SO HOT THAT SHE SHRIEKED WITH PAIN

(Love, which should be a joy, the highest joy, is associated with the deepest submission. The embarrassing thing about pornography is not at all being reminded of your lust or the lust you may have missed, but that it reminds you a bit too clearly that lust is

120

subordinate to power in the world we live in. After the poor
Marquis, who simply viewed without comprehension what he
saw, no one has ventured further into the matter. *Encore un
effort, citoyens!*)

HELPLESS, SHE FELT HOT LIQUID OOZE FROM HER
WIMPERING VAGINA: HER HIPS GLIDED IN TWISTING
MOTIONS AGAINST HER WILL, SHE FELT HER WHOLE
WOMB STIFFEN AND RISE WITH THE PAIN. STILL THE
HAND RESTED, FAR DARKER THAN ANY BLACK
MAN'S HAND, BLACK AS ANTHRACITE, COMPLETELY
STILL ON HER BRASSIERE CUP.
THE ROOM WAS COMPLETELY QUIET.

We begin again. We will never give up.

So I had got as far as my being in Berlin, for months just as
deaf and dumb, as much asleep as King Sigismund III's well-
embalmed corpse in its sarcophagus in the castle of Cracow. I
have experienced such deaths a good many times, but this was
one of the worst. For a couple of weeks, the distance between
that intelligent do-gooder who wrote articles and recorded radio
programs and me was absolutely astronomical.

And then that damn picture in the outhouse at Ramnäs—that
is important. A lightly clad, appetizing couple flee from a burst
glass bubble in a burning laboratory, followed by a long-bearded
Emperor Ming, who will cut his throat if he can't shoot them
with his raygun.

My own situation began to bother me. I began to break out
into a cold sweat on the subway. For a couple of weeks, I had the
strange phobia that I would faint or go crazy when I was out on
the street. Panic was not so very far away.

My daydreams began to be occupied more and more with that
old picture.

(Is "occupied" the right word for what a drowning man does
with the straw?)

The picture, which must have been clipped out of a magazine, is pinned up with four shiny thumbtacks on the wall of resiny pine wall, a little torn on the right side.

It was still hanging there well into the fifties.

Then the house was sold.

It is interesting to see how bourgeois values penetrate every inch of your being all throughout life, although long ago you thought you had seen through your own abilities.

I often wonder what year the petit bourgeois in me was ready, at what age I had learned to obey and be clever. Ten years? Five years? At what age did *cleverness*—I mean, the need to be somebody in someone else's scale of values—come?

Once, around the time of the Battle of Stalingrad, that is, in December 1942, I walked on a flowerbed. Of course the flowerbed was covered by dense, thick snow. It was frozen solid, so that a tank column could have passed over it without leaving the slightest trace.

The flowerbed belonged to the school where I was in kindergarten at the time, and it was strictly forbidden to walk in the flowerbed, even in the middle of December.

I happened to put a boot a fraction of an inch into it and was caught at once by a group of small, ambitious, bright schoolmates from another class who held onto me and dragged me over to their teacher. She took a firm grip on my wrist with a thin, very cold hand

NOW SHE UNDERSTOOD THAT THE WEAK THUMPING SOUND SHE HEARD WAS THE BEAT OF A HEART THAT CONTRACTED ONLY TWO OR THREE TIMES A MINUTE. SHE COULDN'T SUPPRESS A VIOLENT SHUDDER, WHICH RAISED ROUGH GOOSEBUMPS ON HER BARE SHOULDERS

and led me to my own teacher, and you can imagine, the nasty old ladies didn't give up until they had decided that I was to get a

B in conduct for the term just because I had put one foot into a hard-frozen flowerbed. That, of course, caused alarm when I got home.

The whole thing is a trifle. It happened at a time when people in the countries around us were whipped to death without having done anything at all. I met one of those teachers some twenty-five years later when I was buying a watercolor from her brother, who was an excellent landscape painter. It turned out, of course, that she was a nice old woman with starched cuffs and a drip-catcher under the spout of her teapot. She politely pretended that she had lively memories from that period when I went to school, but she didn't remember me at all.

What is interesting rests on an entirely impersonal level. First of all, they didn't want feet in the flowerbed. Second, they needed to have a few B's in conduct, so that their statistics wouldn't seem strange.

What is interesting is that they *chose* me. I was the right type to be chosen.

It could have turned into a career, if I had had the least bad luck. That B could have followed me into elementary school, and they would have described me as rather unruly. Youth gangs, motorcycle thefts in the fifties, a really cunningly planned raid on a gas station at the beginning of the sixties. Penitentiary. Post office raids when they began to be fashionable in the middle of the sixties. Solitary confinement, black headlines in *Expressen*.

I always read with a kind of collegial interest about robbers who hold banks hostage with machine guns and disappear with millions in cash or who are carried off in front of the TV cameras by heavily armed men.

I don't at all want to claim that I approve of them. I am very much in favor of fighting crime, especially when it takes on icy cold, inhuman forms, such as the other autumn in Norrmalmstorg, when some guy held several people cooped up for a whole week in a vault and threatened to hang them if the police tried to knock him out with gas.

He was crazy of course.

But the type itself I understand very well. I myself am one of those whom they had *chosen*. It was just that at that age I was much too thick-skinned to have caught the hint.

What I mean is that it must have been then that they laid the foundation for my fear, my petit-bourgeois mentality. They taught me that they were serious.

Ever since then, I have been ruled by two kinds of fear: the fear of going crazy and the fear of being without money.

In the fall of 1972, in Berlin, I had plenty of money, more than I had ever had in my entire life, and perhaps that contributed to my fear of going crazy becoming so conspicuous.

The real fear in me is not so much of going crazy but of beginning to *behave strangely*.

I am sitting on the subway with a book on my lap. Around me are all of the Berliners who don't have their own cars, that is to say Turks with their large, elegant, Anatolian mustaches and old colonels' widows with lacemaker's pillows on their laps.

"Now," I think, "now I'll suddenly go crazy, shut up here in this car." It will begin with some sort of odd twitch in my right arm that can't be controlled. Then I will bounce up and around in the car, making strange sounds, pull the panties off the colonel's wife nearest me, with her sewing scissors clip off half the mustache of that Turkish champion wrestler at the door, roll around on the floor in paroxysms, and who knows what else. And the whole fear is of behaving, of looking, odd.

If a committee composed of distinguished psychiatrists could assure me that when I finally do go crazy I will do it in a very discrete, very imperceptible, very temperate way, then by God I would actually feel self-confident, almost secure in face of the whole prospect.

The fear of being without money. That was there all the time in my childhood environment, like a pest in the walls. Among my missions of honor at that time—I am speaking about the forties—was to explain to all bill-collectors that Father was in the army and Mother had gone out.

124

Some of them believed me, others didn't.

My mother's sisters and brothers, with the exception of Aunt Clara of course, were always talking about money. Apart from Clara, there wasn't an aunt who didn't play the lottery every week, always hopeful when she came back from the kiosk in Kyrkbyn with her ticket.

Of my mother's brothers, Stig, of course, was the wildest. He didn't dream like my aunts about a hundred thousand kronor. He dreamed of hundreds of millions for each new patent he registered. And he was really convinced the whole time that someone else was gaining them at his expense. Hence, his patent suits.

The whole family sat ensnared in an economic trap. There wasn't one among them who had any hope of saving more than ten thousand kronor in his passbook in a lifetime.

To rise out of their modest circumstances, their small salaries, their small apartments—not one among them had the slightest chance.

It would have been better for them if they had quit dreaming, quit tormenting themselves with thoughts of money. But they couldn't help poking at this money business, just like the person who has a bad tooth can't help poking at it with his tongue.

In my lifetime I have probably met a few really rich people. Claude Gallimard, a Baron Krupp von Bohlen. A few publishers, some industrialists.

I am completely convinced that they don't spend more than five percent of the time my family spent talking and thinking about money.

I am exactly the same way. I have all of their petty, absurd fixations.

For me, money is the world's best tranquilizer. You can never get too much of it. Nothing (except possibly going crazy) could be so ghastly as to suddenly not have any money at all.

Notice that I am not describing this as a false notion. I think it is a fairly accurate picture of reality. Money *is* the world's best tranquilizer, there *is* nothing worse than to be poor, or, if there is, it would have to be having a terrible illness, yet even for the pain of cancer morphine helps some and you always have the hope of dying, but what do you use as an anesthetic against poverty?

It is no trick to make confessions and publish "recklessly honest" books about yourself as long as you talk about your "problem," your perversions, and the agony of your soul.

A much greater step is to begin to talk about your daydreams. Not everyone does that.

The painter G.—that is, the real painter G., whom I met the other day in her slum apartment where the studio is as narrow as a closet and receives the sparse light from a hundred-foot shaft in a Turkish tenement in Moabit—confided in me that her favorite daydream is that behind a curtain she finds a door she has never noticed before.

She can sit for hours when she is tired and fantasize about how she chisels at the door, and when she finally gets it open there is a large, entirely empty, windowless room inside. The landlord has never discovered that it is there. No one knows about it. And it becomes her own.

She claimed that she can sit through entire bus trips furnishing this unknown room, so that she passes her stop.

My daydreams are forty percent sexual. I fancy how I would seduce, in short sleep with one or another of my girl friends, female acquaintances, women I have seen only fleetingly or not for years. It's a little bit reminiscent of the kind of model simulation that can be worked out in a computer program—take space modules, for example—because sometimes, after I have gone through such a daydream in the smallest detail, I decide not to sleep with that girl in reality, or that female friend, although she might not be opposed to it at all.

The rest of my daydreams deal with how I get money without exerting myself.

In my daydreams, I have received every literary award from

126

the Nobel to the Eva Thulin Memorial at least five times (actually I haven't received a literary prize since 1963: I suspect that is well-deserved punishment). There is not an American guest professorship from Anchorage to Austin that I haven't received on modest terms. Sometimes I pull off neat, bloodless, and humane but very elegant bank robberies.

I don't ever behave so clumsily as those stupid numbskulls in the Penitentiary, with their machine guns and ridiculous teenage antics.

Oh no! I go into the Enskilda Bank's main office on Hamngatan, impeccably fitted by the Nordiska Kompaniet's French tailor and with a tie from Via Condotti, say hello to the guard, walk up to the main cashier, and say:

"Listen, we have a terrible problem over at the Sveavägen branch office. We have to have three million dollars for an air-conditioning firm that's negotiating a deal in Kuwait. Can you lend it to me until tomorrow?"

"Hm," says the bank manager. "Say, I don't think we've met."

"Oh yes, at the Club," I answer, "but perhaps you've forgotten. I am Lars Gustafsson, the new manager of the Sveavägen branch. Do you think you can get together a few dollars for me?"

And so on. When I have made my bold move, I don't do anything absurd with automobiles, trains, and airplanes, like the boys in the Penitentiary do. I put the money in Upland Bank and go home.

No one would ever dream of suspecting such an impractical man as me. If they were to go so far as to cross-examine me, I would slam my fist on the table and say that this is really enough of such nonsense. "You aren't going to begin to suspect Alva Myrdal in the last stiletto murder as well!"

"My fingerprints? Really? Did you get dust in the microscope?"

"Oh really, stop! I was there that same morning and put fifteen kronor into the account for earthquake victims in Peru, it's no trick to check that."

"The manager? Ask him to describe how I was dressed! Do you

think I'm able to buy things at the Nordska Kompaniet's French designer shop? Oh, the Nordska Kompaniet's English designer shop. I thought that one had closed. Oh, it's the French one that is closed. Well, you'll have to excuse me, but I don't know much about men's tailors. I'm a workingman, not a snob. If you continue like this any more, my good man, I'll have to write to the judicial ombudsman. High fashion tailors, ridiculous! Tomorrow morning I'll report in *Expressen* on what interrogations are like in this place. I'll have quite a bit to say about being cross-examined on whether the Nordska Kompaniet's English designer shop is closed.

"What was that—excuse me? Hm. Yes. Yes, good-bye now."

What do I need the money for? Nothing. I want it to calm my nerves. And I might possibly do something about the boiler. It's not working so well.

Daydreams. You can't understand this civilization if you don't see that the greater part of it consists of daydreams.

AND THAT THIS COUNTRY IS OCCUPIED: THEY HAVE INFECTED MY DAYDREAMS, AND IN A MORE PRIMITIVE STATE THEY WOULD LOOK COMPLETELY DIFFERENT

My friend B., a young promising playwright, calls me at one o'clock in the morning and reports that he has been gypped out of quite a few thousand marks by an unusually unscrupulous theater agent. He's gone to a lawyer, and the lawyer says that it's futile. The laws don't exist to do justice, they exist mainly to preserve social tranquility. That is, they exist to protect theater agents.

"Didn't you understand that before?" I say. "I thought everyone learned that as a child, given our social class."

B. says that he has always told others that is the way it is, but never dared to take it seriously. In other words, he never thought it could happen to him.

B. has now been awake since eleven o'clock and been pondering what he should do. He was cheated out of about ten thousand marks. Now he has decided that he is going to steal impersonally and dispassionately double the amount wherever he can, in banks, in stores, wherever it does not affect an individual person.

My first reaction is to warn him. "Such things never turn out right." Then it occurs to me that he should without a doubt be allowed to make a decision in this matter himself. Probably it will work out just fine, most crimes of that type often do turn out well, and it will be very good for his personal development. It will give him a new feeling of freedom.

As a rule, crime pays excellently if it is done on a sufficiently grand scale. In the days following the Krueger bankruptcy, a young star attorney went into Krueger's bank in Stockholm where the confused, panic-stricken management was sitting, waiting for the police and contemplating suicide.

"I am the government investigator," he said. "I must ask you to hand over the securities. The gentlemen may leave now."

Not only did this man probably succeed in getting hold of a large portion of the concern's assets, but barely two months passed before the government *was* actually persuaded to commission him as the government investigator.

Loaded with the assets of some tens of thousands of Swedish small savers, this gentleman discreetly withdrew. I hardly think there is a single order, except possibly the Royal Order of the Serafim, by which this man hasn't been honored.

I am convinced that he is for law and order.

The retired old man who intends to tuck an extra package of frozen fishsticks in his coat at the supermarket screws up the job, is taken out onto the street, and has a heart attack for fear of the court proceedings.

His real mistake, of course, is his moderation.

There is not a great distance between him and those guys in the Penitentiary, with their rubber masks and stupid machine guns, their pathetic lower-class dialects and their worm's view of society.

None of them has any idea of how criminal acts can be successfully carried out. There was a gang that in the space of just over one day overthrew Chile's legally elected government, laid waste the Presidential Palace with fighter planes, arrested half the civil servants, murdered about a thousand people, and gained absolute, total power over the state before the sun went up the next morning.

What did *Der Abend* write the next day?

ALLENDE'S GOVERNMENT FAILS

That's the way to turn a trick. With a little luck, this book will end up one fine day in the prison library in the Penitentiary or the Tillberga prison, and then I hope that you start to think when you read this passage, boys.

Okay. You sit and wonder about the next job. Practically speaking, you have the scenario ready, don't you? I don't want to interfere, but let me just point out that the next job will probably be just as wretchedly unpretentious and crude as the previous one, which was borrowed from the latest childish American TV series, complete with stockings over the face and cars waiting at the sidewalk and a funny attempt to take the car across the river by ferry.

You'll never get out of the playground that way, boys.

I have no idea how your next job should be set up, but this much I can say: there would be a rather clear sign it was a big job, an infallible sign.

If the next job hits Scandinaviska Enskilda Bank, all the newspaper reports the next day would be about like this:

SCANDINAVIKSA ENSKILDA BANK FAILS

If you are certain you can manage it, then I absolutely think you should go through with it. We will see each other at next year's Oscar Awards or at the next royal banquet, and then we can wink at each other under the crystal chandeliers. I will see you in the royal box at the track, and then we will wave to each other, if the ladies' big blue hats are not in the way too much.

But if you are not certain you can manage it, boys, then I absolutely think you should take a job at "United Laundries" as drivers when you get out. Nice uniforms and rather pleasant working hours. My Uncle Knutte worked for thirty years there, and he thought it was a wonderful company to work for.

Two days, or to be more precise, two nights later, B. calls up again, the young promising playwright. He has been thinking about Rembrandt's *The Man with the Golden Helmet* at the New National Gallery. It is hanging extremely close to a door.

"First of all, I say it's mean to schoolchildren, second, there's a clever little alarm apparatus behind it, very sensitive, with a lever between the backside of the painting and the wall. All you have to do is put the tip of your little finger on the frame and the alarm will go off. I've thought about it. It'll work if you can cause a power failure. Find out where the museum's main circuit breaker is and rent a powerful sports car."

"You already have a buyer, I gather. I mean, at Sotheby's in London it's possible one customer or another has seen Rembrandt's *The Man with the Golden Helmet* before. Of course you can keep it at home in the attic where you live and show it to the girls."

Four days later he calls up again, dumb B.

"I've done it," he says, positively beaming, "now I've gotten my revenge."

"Great," I say, "then we can read about it in the newspaper tomorrow. Did you find the main circuit breaker?"

"Main circuit breaker? Newspaper?"

"Yes."

"Oh. I just went into one of those big stereo shops on Kudamm and exchanged the price tags on two radios. No one noticed it at the cash register. I got a Grundig that should have cost three hundred for one eighty-two fifty.

131

"Fantastic! A unique crime! And next week it'll be the tooth-picks at the cafeteria, I suppose."

I am afraid that playwright B. lacks any sense of irony.

What I'm trying to get at, boys, is that in reality we are broken from the start. *Broken*, you understand. They frightened us too much in the playground when we were young.

They taught us that Jesus will come and get you if we walk in flowerbeds, and I'll be damned if they weren't right.

You hardly manage to get your foot in the flowerbed before Jesus is there, looking you in the white of the eye.

And that's how it went with my daydreams. They go no further than girls and money.

I know few people who have such an extremely paltry spiritual life as I have. It smells like a tenement with a lot of cabbage soup in the hall. They broke me from the beginning. I am one of those poor creatures who think that cleverness is worthwhile. Who try to make themelves important.

Twenty volumes of spiritual life!

Twenty volumes containing the spiritual life I would have had if they had not broken me. That's how it is. And if they had not broken me, that spiritual life would not be sitting and rusting in twenty absurb volumes. It would be here. *Here*, I mean. (I put my index finger between my eyebrows with a gesture more Mediter-ranean than Scandinavian.)

THE ONES WHO ARE FLYING OUT OF THE GLASS BUBBLE ON THE OUTHOUSE AT RÄMNAS: WHERE DO THEY WANT TO GO? WHERE ARE THEY GOING?

Remember that boy who one day learns how to ride a motorcycle and feels, suddenly, that the wind that rushes around him is a wind of freedom, a Monteverdi wind? I suspect the wind is the first sign that our long, gloomy story is beginning to approach those regions where Purgatory stops and the higher circles begin at last.

You understand, I am beginning to suspect that somewhere

THE WIND BLOWS ALL THE WHOLE TIME, PLAYING WITH THE COILS IN VENUS' LONG GOLDEN HAIR

An Intergalactic War III

The double star B 8744 (Smith's catalogue) in Orion has a modest system of planets, known only to very advanced astronomical cultures. The planets are overgrown with only a primitive kind of lichen, not visible to the naked eye. They exist as weak color shifts in the deep red rocks where they are hidden, mainly in crevice formations.

Around the largest of the planets, however, orbit three moons. The middle one is so well in phase with the double star's rotations that it has two dominant forms of life, completely independent of each other.

One lives in strong daylight, is in fact flooded with ultraviolet quartz lamplight from the powerful sun in the double star.

It is not easy to say exactly what sort of life form it is. Pictures from the best probes show what look like very large swarms of larks dancing over a reddish-purple plain.

After precisely twenty-three months, this species dies out and hibernates for two years as microscopic eggs deep down in the reddish-purple bedrock.

The strong sun goes down for twenty-three months, and up comes the very faint red. Shadows lengthen, everything that had just been so clear and plain and illuminated suddenly becomes nothing but a world of horrors.

Then life form number two emerges on the planet, looking like huge, damp blankets. They live on tiny animals that they chase down, then they lie on top of them, suffocating and dissolving them.

Just a few weeks after the new phase, they are full-grown and rustle around in the feeble light from the two other wandering green moons.

They get their bearings by means of a high, piping sound which is said to have made the few scientists who have visited the place go mad.

134

Here in the red darkness, in a rapidly pitched dome of indestructable quartz crystal, the Galactic Defense Committee met and prepared its definitive plan.

It was not a particularly ideal spot. The strongly illuminated dome turned out to exercise a colossal attraction on the now fully grown blankets, and with blind zeal they flapped and crept over the quartz structure.

It was a weak sound, but troublesome nonetheless.

"The quartermaster general could have chosen a less idiotic place," sighed the First Lord of Space as he leaned over the sheaf of papers in front of him for the tenth time.

"So," the reporting officer continued with an impatient look at the ceiling, "*The Peace Race* is an East European bike race run every year in the middle of May from Prague to Berlin to Warsaw.

"Hundreds of cyclists participate. On the sixth day, the race always passes Cracow, right under the royal castle and cathedral. My plan is based on this circumstance.

"We eliminate one racer and exchange him with one of our own agents, who we'll make sure ends up in the lead pack.

"When they pass below the hill with the cathedral and Sigismund's sarcophagus, we'll strike.

"Quite simply, it can't fail."

The First Lord of Space looked thoughtfully at the ceiling.

"I ALWAYS DREAMED ABOUT SUCH SICKENING BLANKETS AS A CHRYSALIS," HE THOUGHT

A Letter to My Friend Zwatt

Dear Zwatt:

I can see you very clearly as you read this letter I am writing to you now. You are sitting in your grandmother's comfortable chair in your little parlor in Grunewald where there always seems to be sunlight, because there are so many windows facing in so many directions. You are sitting there surrounded by your books and your telephone and your red teapot that never manages to cool off. And you have drawn up your narrow pretty legs under yourself in the chair, and between your big lively eyes a small, ill-humored crease is just forming now, as if the sun had gone behind the clouds, but just for a moment.

I remember very well the first time I noticed your large, unusual eyes.

It was at the opening of an exhibition of some kind, early in the autumn of 1972. I was standing and talking with the Polish exile writer W., a square little man with a square white beard to boot and those high temples you only see on Polish aristocrats and my Uncle Stig.

Who does he remind me of? Now I know! King Sigismund III of Poland, of course, as he is depicted on one of the six portraits in the collection at Gripsholm Castle.

"Look, there's an unusually beautiful woman," W. said to me.

"Say it out loud," I said. "If we're lucky, she'll hear us!"

"Voilà une beauté merveilleuse," W. roared, so that he might have been heard out on the street.

I think you were actually watching us very thoughtfully for a moment.

But in reality, it would still not be until the following year that we became friends.

Dear Zwatt, now I am writing to you.

In Sweden, in December, there is a time when the grass becomes as brittle as glass. No snow has come yet, but the frost is in the

136

ground. After midnight, well before sunrise, whole fields are covered by a fine layer of frost, and it rustles when you walk through the long-since dead grass.

On such a December morning in 1956, I participated in a military maneuver out on a flat, desolate plain called Norra Uppland. We had been awakened at two o'clock in the morning, and now we had halted at a fork in the road far out on the plain.

I had crept down into a ditch to sleep a little, a very dry, comfortable, hard-frozen ditch. I lay on my back with my arms under my head and, looking up into the starlight that occasionally broke through the frost in the blades of grass, thought how very flimsy man is.

Yes, just that—*flimsy*. Outside me—a great, bottomless darkness filled with stars; inside—a bottomless, slowly pulsating darkness. Between these two darknesses—that membrane, thin as a soap bubble, where images arise.

And it is only there, in that thin membrane, that we exist.

And at the same time, in that membrane somehow are all the other people.

Good God, what impractical thoughts! And yet it is only thoughts of that kind which can finally convince me that there is some meaning in my existence.

The whole, pitiful petit-bourgeois mentality—the greed, the curse of cleverness that history together with the fate of having grown up in a tenement on the outskirts of Västerås have forced on me—tells me that I should not be thinking such thoughts. *They are not for me.*

G., a girl I know slightly, got a nasty toothache in her upper jaw the other day. She went to the dentist. He examined it. "It's not a pretty picture," he said. "It requires oral surgery and it's a very difficult procedure. Do you have money?"

G. had no money. "Yes, then unfortunately I can't do anything," said the dentist. G. then raced around for a couple of days to social welfare organizations to gather the three or four hundred marks needed from her before they would free her from unbearable pain.

What is the moral difference between mistreating a person to earn four hundred marks and letting a person suffer unbearable pain, again for four hundred marks?

I went to the dentist that same week. "There's one cavity in a molar, plus others," I said when I went in. No one asked me for money in advance, the bill was ridiculously cheap, everything functioned in a well-oiled manner.

I think it took more than thirty years before I discovered the protective net that surrounds some people and is lacking for most.

Of course, it is not my modest economic assets that are being rewarded. It is my language, my correct grammar.

And of course, this language functions not only as a signal, a membership badge in that small group which is always treated well.

What causes my language to be rewarded is that it holds the possibility of control.

It is the kind of language that enables someone to articulate for himself what may be done to him.

I remember how it was when I was a little schoolkid and did not have this ability.

As a rule, what we are able to articulate they do not impose on us. What we are not able to articulate, they do impose.

They imposed something on me I am unable to articulate.

Therefore, this Sigismund whom I have for so long poked fun at lies dry and dead in his coffin, covered with spiderwebs.

Noticeably often you see how Jewish women put up their hair behind in a peculiar way, leaving their ears free. You do it too, sometimes, without thinking about it.

On the other hand, my Grandmother Emma, who was not Jewish at all, also used to wear her hair that way.

These symbols we create ourselves, these structures that repeat themselves because we want them to repeat, interchangeable pieces of a puzzle, are so remarkable.

I always talk to women who wear their hair that way with the greatest candor and seriousness, because Grandmother Emma was the only person who succeeded in winning my confidence when I was five or six years old.

That isn't so strange, you say, such impressions exist. Sure.

What is strange, though, is that it makes sense. It works.

They *are* the right people to go to. In this way, we create a world where a moment ago there was none. We establish values, functioning forms, grammar, and logic out of accidental circumstances, and after a while they are not accidental circumstances anymore but the whole of reality.

I remember sitting once in a café several years ago, in Berlin, by the way, and speaking about how difficult, how remote happiness is, and how an extremely small portion of your life you can really refer to as being happy.

And just then, a completely happy person walked by outside the window's green half-curtain. An obese woman in her fifties or sixties, with sausage-case stockings slipping down a bit on her formless legs. And one of the happiest smiles I have ever seen.

"Aren't we demanding too much, if she can be happy and not us," I said to the person I was talking to.

"You're wrong, Lars," she said. "You can't compare your own happiness or unhappiness with someone else's. Every man is his own measure."

I have thought very much about what she said. Coming from such a decidedly democratic person as she is, that is a remarkable utterance, and I think it is absolutely correct.

Dear Zwatt, you know as well as I do how things are in the world. Our cities are becoming more and more uninhabitable, the freedoms the previous century dreamed about are becoming more and more utopian, more a subject for the history of ideas. Not even such a simple thing as the parliamentary system has the least significance anymore for the people who are affected by its decisions. Inexorably, a blinder, more mechanistic capitalism is chewing up one sector of life after the other. The terrible machine is rushing ahead like a tractor-trailer the driver of which has fallen asleep but whose force on the gas pedal steadily increases.

Right in the midst of this catastrophe, we live rather thoroughly contented, so long as our fundamental needs for affection, trust, and someone to listen to us are satisfied.

We would live much worse off in a utopian society, if there were no one there who loved us.

Is that how it is, dear Zwatt? Is our real condition—Paradise, or in the last resort, Hell—something we decide upon ourselves?

And how cynical it is not to ask.

I always have to laugh when I read these psychologistic theories of religion which purport that different peoples and cultures have invented God as some sort of extension or projection of the paternal ego.

Big daddy with a rod and a box of candy!

What a ridiculous, completely superfluous, roundabout way to explain a simple thing.

Why do we need to magnify the paternal ego? It's obvious, I think, that it is our own ego, in cosmic magnification, we are talking about when we say "God."

Each one of us calls himself "I," and with equal right. Only one single person can properly call himself "I"—the one who is talking.

There is simply one solution to the problem, and that is an ego which embraces, which creates the world.

The sovereign ego, imprisoned in its structures, ever repeated. The paralyzed ego, imprisoned in history, which does not allow so much as a millimeter of space for freedom of action, sovereignty, happiness. There is something here that does not fit!—something I do not understand at all. In the last analysis, life

140

consists of our dreams about life, of the meanings we ourselves are able to give them. In the end, life consists of everything, I say *everything*, except simply this: our dreams.

Poor King Sigismund, imprisoned so long in his heavy limestone coffin! Zwatt, my dear, I know what we'll do! We'll give him a chance! We'll release him!

Yes. We'll do that. We'll do it like this:

The Peace Race 1973: The Sixth Stage

Over central Poland's villages and small cities, an ice-cold, drizzling rain had been falling the whole morning.

Nevertheless, there was a good crowd of spectators along the willow-lined avenues when the sixth heat of the Peace Race rushed by. At noon especially, when the factories and businesses had their lunch break, it was almost black with people along the road.

The youngest of the Fåglum brothers had been forced to drop out that morning: he simply had too heavy a cold. For three days he had been suffering, with a pounding heart and fever-fogged eyes, as the avenues flowed together into a single, cursed green tunnel.

The cold, thin rain that had been falling day after day made the asphalt tough to ride on. The cobblestones in the villages shook the racers' stomachs.

Sometimes the entire column—with its escort of cars, peace banners, repair and spare-part vehicles, tightly grouped motor-cycle police, yet more motorcycle police, the long-drawn-out string of racers behind the lead pack—the whole of this mobile and snaking peace demonstration had to brake at a railroad crossing while a groaning, smoking locomotive with countless cars rattled past gates.

When the nuisance had finally gone by in a cloud of coal smoke and lonely clattering, the motorcyclists started up their engines, the lead pack (with their pants glued to their wet thighs) picked up the pace again. Every time the race froze fast in this way at a railroad crossing, the whole competition locked in position, caught like a photograph, only to continue on as before.

The cyclists' thigh muscles hurt like hell at every such interruption in the pouring rain, and there was more than one who asked himself why he had ever chosen to become a bike racer.

The youngest Fåglum, as mentioned before, had dropped out, his brothers were still in the lead pack, as were the Yugoslav Michailov Bogomile, his country's great hope, the Hungarian Stanko Raikowicz, and the East German Ferdinand Forsche, the previous day's leader.

They had taken off at ten o'clock in the morning and had been drafting each other well but without too many discussions and disputes, the lead cyclists knowing well how to utilize the suction of the rainsoaked asphalt to put a decent distance between themselves and the middle of the field.

Everything was going quite well now in the stretches between the railroad crossings, which recurred with deadly monotony. The lead calmly changed gears, no one did anything stupid, the rain continued to fall. Sometimes along a really desolate stretch, a cyclist motioned one of the escort cars over to himself, grabbed a steady hold of the handrail, and took a solitary piss in the rain.

Along the road, it smelled of newly blossomed chestnut trees. It was spring, but, as often in Poland, nasty, apt to give you a cold.

It was a long haul until the afternoon and a long way to Cracow, the final goal for this stage.

Mile after mile passed without anything really happening.

No one noticed the new rider in black pants and a gleaming yellow shirt with the club sign "ANDROMEDA" until he had already been hanging at the back of the lead pack for a long while. He wore the number 666 on his back and pedaled with a calm, springy kick. Where was he from? He had clearly worked his way up to the lead pack through that last long avenue of birches.

"Who in the hell is that," said the man in the lead escort car. For there had been, in fact, no number 666.

Withold Gork from the bicycle club Andromeda in Katowice. None of the organizers had ever heard of that bicycle club. But Poland has many such clubs.

The black rider was evidently using protective glasses, the journalists noticed, and had a club cap pulled down all the way to his eyebrows.

He seemed to be in excellent shape, but obviously did not care to take over the lead and just coasted at the back of the pack.

After a while, he got a sign from the lead car to let loose, and he seemed to do it with the greatest of ease. Ferdinand Forsche dropped back, relieved, and the man from Andromeda placed himself in the lead. The wind had increased a little now, moving uneasily in the crowns of the willows. The groups of school-children along the road seemed ever sparser and more melancholy with the small pennants in their hands.

The newcomer was an excellent lead rider. He had an ability that bicycle racers appreciate: he maintained a fantastically even pace. He held at exactly the upper limit of what the riders were capable of in that weather, without making even the slightest microscopic jerk, and when the pack was clocked for the next half-hour, it turned out that it had maintained a speed seven miles faster than the previous half hour.

"Fantastic," said Gerber, the leader of the East German team. "He'll be dangerous later in the afternoon. But who the hell *is* Withold Gork? I never heard of the guy before. And what's this Andromeda in Katowice?"

He looked wildly through his program, but there was no other information than that Withold Gork was registered as number 666. What the hell had he been doing with himself on the previous stages?

Gork, it seemed, had been there all along on the five previous stages, finishing strangely enough each time at exactly that stage's mathematical average. "Strange coincidence," thought Gerber.

Around three o'clock in the afternoon, it began to become quite clear that Gork from Katowice was the sensation of the day, predestined to be the winner of the sixth stage. For the last fifteen miles, he had headed the lead pack without interruption, against an icy, ever heavier wind, and simply rejecting with a shake of the head every more or less generous offer to be relieved. The guy must have been incredibly stubborn and well trained. What the hell had he been trying to do with himself on the previous five stages, when he had obviously been satisfied with coming in exactly at the middle, so exactly as a matter of fact that each time his pace had agreed with the stage's mathematical average. Old Peace Race habitués just shook their heads.

"It'll never last to the finish line," they thought.

Later in the afternoon, just outside of Cracow, the sun finally broke out and the rain stopped. There were quite a few people beside the road, and along the whole approach that gradually winds below the hill where the castle and cathedral lie, there hung gay red streamers with such slogans as:

CRACOW WELCOMES THE PARTICIPANTS IN THE PEACE RACE

and there were quite a few groups of schoolchildren and small Boy Scouts in neat red bandanas. The afternoon news on the radio had mentioned the exciting turn of events that the sixth stage had taken. A young Pole, Withold Gork, from the Andromeda club in Katowice, had surprisingly taken the lead, and several of the commentators predicted that this was the beginning of a new Polish era of greatness in bicycle racing. The commentators had even been able to say a little about Gork's place of work, a machine shop in Katowice, while the television showed Gork's comrades at their lathes, where they were enthusiastically following their fellow worker's progress on the radio. All that had attracted many more people to the race, and the traffic police were warning the spectators not to walk too far out onto the course.

At the finish stood the girl with the wreath, a dark girl with fabulous brown eyes, clad in a folk costume and ready with the

145

garland. The loudspeakers that had been strung up came on abruptly and with a terrible metallic echo began to report that Withold Gork had made a fantastic breakaway four miles from the finish. It was perfectly unbelievable, he was already two miles in front of the others.

The television showed dramatic silhouettes of this phenomenon from Katowice, still steaming wet after the rain but now in the sunshine, in a fantastic final spurt. Could he last? Clearly, he did not seem the least bit tired. On the contrary, the distance between Gork and the lead pack now increased with surprising speed.

A great new epoch in the history of Polish bicycle racing apparently was at hand.

Gork was still picking up speed. It was already clear that if he could keep it up, he would have the best time for the sixth stage in the history of the Peace Race.

At every new report, the jubilation grew at the finish line below the castle in Cracow, and around Withold Gork, the lone hero fighting up the big hills toward Cracow, a spring wind roared with ever greater strength, the sun shone more warmly—in spite of everything, wasn't spring finding its way down through the rapidly scattering cloud cover?

Now there were just two miles left to the finish. From far down the highway, a rising, completely animal-like cheering from the spectators could already be heard.

Withold Gork from Katowice was on his way to setting a course record on the sixth stage of the Peace Race.

What now followed has become known as one of the great scandals in the noble history of Polish bicycle racing.

The sixth stage of the Peace Race in May 1973 was won, as everyone knows, by the repeated East German champion Ferdinand Forsche, who set a new stage record for the stretch.

As some people know, Forsche became the object of a number of unpleasant demonstrations at the finish, afterward dealt with in an exhaustive, strictly secret exchange of letters between, respectively, the East German foreign office and sports department, the incident gradually being dismissed as malicious rumors.

It was obvious that Forsche had not been expected to be the winner of the stage. His arrival produced a certain confusion at the finish. Forsche unfortunately seems to have tripped over his bicycle so badly that the handlebars caught him below the right eye, but this resulted, however, only in a black eye.

Poland's favorite, young Withold Gork, because of a sudden pulled muscle, was forced to drop out only a few hundred yards from the finish, as all newspaper readers know.

A few days after the Peace Race had passed Cracow, a strange rumor spread through the city that Withold Gork had gone the wrong route on the final stretch itself, and instead of riding to the finish, had continued up the hill "at an insane pace." This rumor can be thoroughly contradicted. Gork did it himself in a newspaper interview that same evening:

IT WAS CLOSE BUT UNFORTUNATELY I DIDN'T MAKE IT, SAYS GORK

Of course, no one can ride "at an insane pace" up the castle hill in Cracow, least of all when he in that way loses the chance to inaugurate a new epoch in the history of Polish bicycle racing.

But many TV viewers will remember the picture of this resolute young Pole, with his black protective glasses pulled down and his black cap, fighting for Poland and the Andromeda club in the strong spring wind, mile after mile at the same stone-hard pace, only to be deprived of the winner's wreath in the last few minutes of the stage by an odd muscle tear.

Zygmunt Spaciruje Znowu?

ZYGMUNT SPACIRUJE ZNOWU?

Awkward intermezzo in Cracow
Sigismund's sarcophagus empty

Cracow, Thursday—An occurrence in Cracow's Cathedral, as strange as it is hard to explain, was reported to the local police authorities on Thursday morning by Cathedral's bailiff, Dr. Zbigniew Lanovsky. In connection with a restoration commission taking an inventory of the cathedral, the sarcophagus that has for so long contained the earthly remains of King Sigismund III was opened on Thursday. It was affirmed that the sarcophagus was empty.

"What is strange," according to Commissioner Pryzbyzevski, head of the Third Department's Criminal Division," is that the sarcophagus does not show the slightest trace of tampering. It is undoubtedly an act of some extremist group of Restorationists, and we have every expectation of picking up the track of the perpetrators. An arrest can be expected within the next few hours."

"Fortunately," says Professor Jan Piatowski, manager of the University's laboratory for the restoration of church art, "the perpetrators did not cause any damage at all to the sarcophagus, a masterpiece of Baroque sculpture."

"So nonexistent is the damage, as a matter of fact," adds Professor Piatowski, "that you would think the sarcophagus had been opened from the inside."

(*Trybuna Ludu*, May 5, 1973)

Portrait of the Inner Life of a Liberal: The Middle of the Seventies

Okay. Take it easy, boys! Don't shoot! He's coming out, it seems, voluntarily. Just take it easy. You can put your safeties on, boys! Up with the visors! Undo the bulletproof vests! A-ten-hut! Order arms! Bring out with the chow wagon and the handcuffs!

He's coming now, voluntarily.

Okay, boys! I'm coming.

BUT WHAT IS HE GOING TO USE A SILVER TRAY FOR? DOES HE THINK HE IS A WAITER? THE GUY IS NUTS, COMPLETELY NUTS:

Okay. I'll tell the truth. Between this page and the previous one I have been thinking seriously for several weeks whether I perhaps should drop the whole business. There are other things to do. Open a little workshop in Norberg, for example, where everything would be repaired that no one else wanted to try repairing, now that everything which cannot be repaired is thrown out, from TV sets to lungs.

I could take in old Mora clocks that summer guests buy at auctions and remove the rust from them, and I could repair pumps, electric sump pumps, and mechanical toys. I am actually very good at carefully taking apart small, rusty machines, oiling them and putting in a spring or a locknut here and there, and getting them to run again.

I could make just as good a living at that, and I do not have any real social ambitions anymore. I already know what luxury hotels look like and corporate dining rooms, and there is not an embassy where I have not eaten caviar at least once.

That is what I was thinking. But now, in any case, I have decided to take up my authorship again. Authorship.

Damn it, you begin to see how the story could end, that's clear as day, isn't it?

The other evening, I was visiting some nice German students, and we were sitting there in the usual cooperative apartment below the usual giant poster of Che Guevara, which is now beginning to be exchanged for an equally large reproduction of a drawing by Aubrey Beardsley. (Beauty is the only thing that lasts.)

And we sat there, as I mentioned, and drank two or three bottles of wine, which to tell the truth I had the honor of paying for—I have begun to reach the age where they expect me to pay for the bottles if they are going to sit at my feet—and I had just told the remarkable story about the teacher Janeberg in Västerås.

Janeberg, a high school teacher in Västerås, a little lively man, is standing one fall morning at the blackboard and talking about the province of Skåne's economic geography, when he suddenly catches sight of a nasty black spot on one of his wrists. It does not go away if you pick at it; on the contrary, it hurts like hell and seems to be filled with liquid.

Janeberg, who is a bit hypochondriac, goes to the school doctor during lunch. The doctor shakes his head. He has never in his thirty-year practice seen anything like it. "You'll get over it," he says, "but if you want, I can send you to the Central Hospital." "Do that," says Janeberg, who is somewhat nervous by nature.

At the hospital, he sits around the whole morning and then is admitted. The head physician screws up his eyes behind his gold-rimmed bifocals, picks at his big red nose, and says: "That's odd. There's only one diagnosis, but it's so unbelievable that I don't dare to make it. It's surely something harmless, but I'm going to get a sample in any case and send it to the Bacteriology Institute in Uppsala." And when he notices that Janeberg becomes a little pale, he adds: "I'm completely convinced it's nothing at all. This is a purely routine measure."

"Is it *that*," says Janeberg. "It can't really be?"

"No. Well, no, it *isn't that*, in any case," says the head physician. "It *isn't*. Do you have any reason to suspect something like *that*?"

Eight days pass. Three new bluish blisters break out on Janeberg. At the Bacteriology Institute in Uppsala a lab assistant leans over his microscope for the sixth time and says to himself: "I must be going crazy, I must be going crazy."

He calls the professor. The professor leans over the microscope, breathes heavily (he is an old, asthmatic professor, rather confounded by having been disturbed, but one of the world's greatest authorities in his field), and whistles, makes a fine adjustment, smiles and sings for quite a while. When he finally looks up from the microscope, he grins a beaming boyish grin at his assistant and says:

"Will you be so kind as to call the Department of the Interior, the County Administration in Västmanland, the Military Commander in the Fourth Military District, the Royal Medical Board, the School Superintendant, and the Minister of Justice and ask them to come over here."

"???"

"We have, you see, a case of the Black Death here."

As far as Janeberg is concerned, he was completely restored to health after ten days of rigid penicillin treatment. No one else had ever come down with the Black Death in Västmanland since the fourteenth century.

But it is conceivable, I think, as a small reminder of the trouble you can run into.

The young people thought so, too, and then we played—that is to say, someone went to the record player and played—something over a huge loudspeaker that turned out to be Beethoven's third Leonore Overture.

I must have been a little tired or intoxicated, or perhaps both a little tired and a little intoxicated, for when we came to that trumpet signal, that distant, liberating trumpet—you could say, the original, unspoiled individualist and liberal signal in European art, one which does not say a damn thing about the necessity of purging kulaks to bring about the kingdom of happiness on earth, a signal that is completely indifferent to party disciplines, five-year plans, and shots in the back of the neck, and says that freedom exists: YOU CAN DO WHAT YOU WANT. "Good God," I thought, "that's what I've been talking about all the time! That's exactly what I mean! Good God, I'm *liberal* at heart!"

LOVE ME, I AM A LIBERAL!

Around the corner, there is a better life for us all. Yes.

I am afraid that that will not help much.

In India, there are still places where all first-born children are turned over to a Moslem cult and wrapped in bandages, so that they lose the ability to move and their brains do not develop. They are then sold as beggars, because they are so easy to carry. No Indian government has made the slightest effort to change this situation.

The latest investigations show that working-class conditions in England are for the most part exactly the same as when Engels described them. Rats swarm in workers' dwellings in Manchester and Leeds quite as much as in the 1860s. Is there a single place in the world where you can claim even one social advance that had not already been realized by the end of the eighteenth century?

The ideas of freedom that the great parties could proclaim in England and Prussia in the 1890s no political party today would dream of presenting seriously. On their perches, some long-haired extremists dare to claim on mimeographed sheets that it is right for you to have your personal opinions protected from the police.

Technical advancement! Phooey! I put it the way John Stuart Mill does: Is there a single example of a machine that has made life easier for a single person?

152

I am beginning to feel like the geography teacher Janeberg. The plague exists everywhere around us, but I am the only one it strikes.

From Sudan come pictures of calves starved to death. They lie with their long, wrinkled necks twisted into pathetic positions against the parched and cracked clay.

That little clique of planning experts, guest lecturers, and writers on their way to conferences fly around in jumbo jets, stay at air-conditioned Hilton hotels, and sit at meetings. All the while, they run into acquaintances at airports, and it makes them think the world is terribly small—which it undeniably is, if by the world you mean a narrow social circle of some ten thousand people. And sitting in their conference rooms and in their Hilton hotels, they do not understand that everything they see is just a stage set, that behind the screens the world is rotting to pieces, that it is the same chaotic, brutal, crumbling world as at the end of the Roman Empire, only a thousand times larger, a thousand times more brutal, and that the darkness is actually increasing, rapidly, like a tidal wave.

LOVE ME, I AM A LIBERAL

The other day, I met an agreeable German professor of philosophy from Heidelberg, a pleasant guy, well educated, who knew Hegel, practically speaking, by heart.

He was going to go to Calcutta in November. There is naturally nothing remarkable about someone going to Calcutta. I myself am going to Australia in March; so, he is going to Calcutta in November—Calcutta, where the dirty brown river flows past the quays full of half-burned corpses, partially chewed by dogs and rats; Calcutta, where beggars are cultivated in cages like cauliflower to develop the right stature and be fit for their owners to carry along . . . to this Calcutta he was going to go to lecture on German idealist philosophy.

153

LOVE ME, I AM A LIBERAL

I am not criticizing him, of course. I am only brooding. There is currently something that I am beginning to become more convinced of, namely, that we are in an insane asylum. I am entirely too sober, without fantasies, calculating and wise really to thrive in the crisis section of an insane asylum. I would rather sleep a sleep of many hundreds of years in a sarcophagus, blanketed with cobwebs and plaster and with dead spiders under my eyelids, than allow myself to be drawn into this howling, screaming, sighing, dangerous insane asylum.

YOU SHOULDN'T HAVE AWAKED ME. THAT WAS STUPID OF YOU TO WAKE ME

That is about where the trumpet in Leonore comes into play. The voice of common sense, a signal that obviously comes from a place outside the prison (not from God but from common sense), that says: All right, that's enough, boys, the joke's over, now you better get your goddamn act together, things can't go on this way. You damn well better look at what you're throwing away, what it is you could've become if you'd really chosen.

Around the old lock in Färmansbo, you hear water everywhere. It is an ancient canal, already built at the beginning of the eighteenth century, demolished and fallen into ruin, rebuilt again. In the summer, excursion boats go through the huge, high, copper-green lock gates that hang from great iron buckles set in heavy black stone.

In my childhood, there was no traffic through the lock, the gates were too rotten. From the end of the forties to the beginning of the sixties, there was hardly a boat that went through it.

I occasionally used to make my way overland down to the lock through the dense greenery, through the low bushes with all the adders, through the high grass and under the tall trees, then on to

154

the actual spot where the stream divides, one part canal and the other not (with huge boulders around which the water forms eddies). I would sit down on a large, smooth stone bollard and listen to the water around me and see how it moved in black whorls and how a sort of humus-smelling scum formed like a peculiar whipped cream on the top step of the stairs that go down to the sluice itself, where the boats once went.

And used to sit there for hours, with or without a fishing pole, and look down into the black eddies, with black fourteen-year-old eyes, and ask myself what the hell they really thought I was supposed to do or accomplish in the world.

AND THAT IS THE SINGLE LIBERAL THING IN ME

Okay, boys. Take it easy. He's coming out now.

The Painter G. Makes Some Progress

"What's fantastic," the painter G. said to herself, leaning over the coarse, rustic desk of a very dark oak that adorned the spot in front of the window in the country inn where she was living for the moment, "the fantastic thing is that this remarkable civilization could develop so far and find such original solutions to every possible problem without ever discovering so simple a thing—that writing paper doesn't actually have to look like a well-used old blanket. I simply just don't understand how they went about it!"

She had her reasons to be dissatisfied. The grayish, very coarse paper that lay in front of her was so much like felt to the point of being unbearable. She cursed the bad luck that she hadn't at least taken along a ballpoint pen when she left her apartment in Moabit that night . . .

. . . how long had she actually been away? Three days, fourteen days, ten years, it was absolutely impossible to figure, since she was in a different time not subject to the usual conditions.

Now she was forced to use a disgusting pen with a steel tip, the kind she had not held since elementary school, and at every new thick fiber in the feltlike paper, the wretched ink spurted in a long elegant curve out over the sheet.

It really is not easy to make travel sketches under such circumstances.

Yet, there was so much she wanted to describe: the strange, archaic villages with their narrow streets and high-stepped gables; the dark pubs with their taciturn, fat waiters; the strange smell of an incredibly strong beeswax, unfamiliar to her, that seemed to permeate all the buildings, an aroma that was in this room, too, for that matter.

Could you ever get used to it, if you were actually forced to live here?

Otherwise, things did not seem quite so awful as she had imagined. The landscape was friendly if somewhat monotonous

156

in its friendliness, apparently quite full of lakes, and very normal ones too—she had even seen some men in waders fishing for trout with dry flies at the head of a small stream a couple of days ago, and very normal trout, it seemed. The leafy trees, mostly oak and maple, evidently had a heavier foliage than in Berlin, but it was also very clear that she was at a markedly more southern latitude. Certain days, especially when the wind came from the south, it actually became quite hot. Perhaps there was a desert to the south?

It struck her time after time that she actually had no idea of how much of the country she had actually seen. How representative was the region where she had traveled around for a few days in an ancient Buick (with a huge dent in one front fender and a frightful smell of gasoline inside the car)? The car had a taciturn chauffeur, a large, very silent man in a leather jacket, with very big eyes, which gave him a strange, doglike appearance. Not especially talkative, he was clearly driving her around following an old routine itinerary for visiting guests, focused mainly on historical sites and picturesque landscape.

There was always a room reserved for her, with a neatly made bed with a soft down comforter, lunches were laid out in small dusky pubs with enchanting views of the mountains at exactly one o'clock in the afternoon. It would have been a rather tiresome, rather touristy program had not the country been so strange.

And a little forbidding, in spite of everything. For example, those archaic towns high up in the mountain passes where they had to stop the Buick in front of sixty-foot copper gates with bizarre ornamentation in high relief twisting over the metal, images of fairy-tale monsters and strange dragons that definitely did not belong to the biology at home. The chauffeur would stop, as I mentioned, in front of the huge, sixty-foot gates and press a button on a little doorbell, and after a couple minutes of waiting, they opened, squeaking on thick hinges, without your actually being able to see who opened them or from where they were opened.

Then came a kind of town that was common in those parts: high, narrow houses, close alleys, façades that showed a very unkind aspect to the street, but always an old woman seated Mediterranean-style in a chair outside and crocheting or knitting at the edge of the sidewalk.

She did not have any real sense of communication with the population. The chauffeur, who spoke excellent German—God only knows where he had learned it; it was very idiomatic but sometimes surprising in the slightly archaic turns of phrase—interpreted all her conversations with the people in a dry and pedantic manner, and it would always be the same uninteresting conversation. Not that they were impolite—on the contrary, everyone seemed courteous and friendly—but uninteresting, so terribly uninteresting.

Yesterday evening, for example, she had attempted a conversation with some men and women, dumpy, somewhat rustic types with pronounced pug noses, who were throwing darts against a board in the inn's crowded bar. It had been precisely the usual, uninteresting exchange she was beginning to get used to, after several dozen of the same kind.

"Are you from these parts?"

"Yes, we live right outside the village."

"Do you often drop in here?"

"Not too often. Well, sometimes. On Friday evenings, mostly."

"This is a rather pretty area."

"Yes. Sure enough."

"Are food prices high around here?"

"Vegetables are very cheap. Mutton is a little more expensive."

"Do you have inflation?"

"?"

"Do the prices often rise?"

"How do you mean, 'rise'?"

"Do the prices get higher from year to year?"

"No. We have never heard of anything like that. Prices have always been the same."

158

"I see. Are the authorities easy to deal with?"

"There aren't many authorities here."

"I mean tax collectors, and—and police, and—and game wardens, and so on."

"Oh yes. Pretty fair. We don't see them very often."

"So, you're satisfied then?"

"We make out all right."

Somehow, she could never really reconcile herself with the idea that for these people living in such a curious world was a matter of course. They considered it obvious. There was something wrong, something terribly wrong, but it was not at all easy to find out what it was.

Now one of those hot winds was blowing outside in the night again, rustling the treetops beyond her window, and putting the curtain into uneasy motion.

"There had to be extremely hot deserts further to the south," she thought. "I'll have to ask to get a look at them."

Two days before, when she was taking a stroll in a little town, mostly to look at some amusing handicraft items of copper that were laid out for spectators on a simple wooden bench outside a shed, she suddenly discovered something else.

The street had very little traffic. At one end sat two old women in black kerchiefs, crocheting and talking to each other from their wooden chairs across one sidewalk to the other, in rather shrill and old-womanish but melodic voices. And at the other end of the street, some middle-aged men with obvious great pleasure were playing boccie with very heavy, coal-black balls. One of them was reading a book between bowls, so the others had to tell him when it was his turn again.

At that moment, it dawned on her. It was so simple, she quite simply could not understand why it had not occurred to her before.

In this entire street scene, there was not a single child! She quickly ran through her memories of cities, villages, people out in the fields, trout fishermen on slippery rocks in swift mountain streams—faces, crowds, conversations.

That was it! Not a single child anywhere!

"Yes, there is one thing I'd like to ask," she said to the doglike chauffeur while the Buick, smelling as usual of gasoline and with a strange squeaking sound in the body, rushed ahead through a very narrow avenue of poplars that was dangerous for traffic, "there is one thing I have been thinking about."

The chauffeur hardly seemed to have heard her. All of a sudden he double-clutched and noisily downshifted behind a hay-wagon that had the bad luck of meeting another such right at the curve of the exit from the avenue, and there was no opportunity to be heard.

She made a new attempt on the next straightaway, but just then there was a rattling, old blue bus with lots of baskets of chips and caged chickens on the roof that had to be passed. She had a subtle feeling that, without saying it right out, he wanted to make it clear to her that he was not going to assume any responsibility for traffic accidents if she was going to disturb him all the time with her dumb questions.

On the whole, the man was more unsophisticated than seemed permissible.

The one time she had succeeded in getting into a conversation with him was while they were waiting for a flat tire to be fixed at a simple tire workshop in back of a garage, and then he had enlarged on a remarkable geographical theory based on the idea that men actually live on the inside of a sphere, with the stars in the middle. This had alarmed her a little, until she realized that had to be the normal view in a corner of the world which somehow actually lay inside the earth.

But in any case, there were no children. Once you discovered that, you missed them everywhere.

160

"Presumably," she wrote, while the ink spurted uncontrollably here and there over the feltlike paper, which was the only kind they had been able to offer her, "presumably the absence of children in these parts is an aspect of another phenomenon, namely, that you never, no matter in what direction you drive across the landscape, see a cemetery. The same phenomenon that has caused the price of butter in this village to remain unchanged for nine thousand years, and nine thousand years ago it went down only by one half percent just because a road tax had been removed, the same phenomenon makes that authorities here don't seem to play the least role."

And since she was quite far down on the page and thought it was time to bring the day's travel sketches to a truly tidy conclusion, she added:

"The most characteristics things about Hell are its idyllic, rather mountainous landscape of lakes and leafy trees, with occasional fiery winds blowing from the south, and the social life's completely petrified, utopian static character."

Very satisfied with herself she got undressed, brushed her teeth carefully, removed her make-up with a cleanser, and blew out the kerosene lamp.

She slept a deep and dreamless sleep.

When she awoke, she found to her surprise that she no longer was alone in the room. Belo was sitting in the chair at the desk, dressed in an elegant, light summer suit, with one leg nonchalantly dangling over the other, paging through her sketches with little satisfied laughs. He was smoking a cigarette in a long amber mouthpiece, which irritated her a bit.

Warm sunlight had been shining in through the curtains for several hours, casting a broad streak of light on the floor.

"Good morning," Belo said.

"Good morning," said the painter G. "Would you be so kind as to put out that awful cigarette? I'm a little sensitive to smoke in my bedroom, especially when I haven't even got out of bed yet."

"Excuse me," Belo said. "I should have thought of that."

"I don't know that I've given you permission to read my sketches, but since you're doing it anyway, I have to say that there was one thing I forgot to write down yesterday evening but which should be there."

"Oh," said Belo, inviting.

"Yes, it's that in Hell, you never once see a bicyclist," the painter G. said soberly.

"No, you're right about that," said Belo. "Here you never do see a bicyclist."

The Last Contract Stipulation

"Well?" said Belo. He moved the tip of his right foot up and down, observing it meditatively.

"What do you mean 'well'?" said the painter G. in a slightly irritated tone of voice you almost could have interpreted as maternal, if anything so strange had been possible.

"I mean: What do you think?"

"It's a very pretty landscape, the population is taciturn but otherwise all right. Apart from a few small things like stationary, the industrial standards are higher than I expected."

"You mustn't forget that we've had war for millennia," Belo dutifully tossed in. "The reconstruction work . . ."

"The other side has damn well had to do it, too," the painter G. snapped back. She was really having an unusually irritable day.

"You have no idea of how great an amount of work has been done down here. You should have seen how it looked after the most recent military actions with Heaven. Our standard of living is presently increasing three times as fast as the U.S.A.'s."

"I believe you, sir," said the painter G. "But that's not what's of concern."

"So, you're disappointed."

"Yes."

"But about what?"

"Everything is so terribly static here. Nothing really happens. There's not even a single child here."

"And no revolutions, plagues, traffic accidents, factory shutdowns, no inflation," Belo said. "What do you think the Utopians have always dreamed about, if not precisely this?"

He extended his hand in a magnificent gesture and was about to knock over the kerosene lamp that was dangerously near him on the desk. Not about to, it actually fell from the edge of the desk, and the painter G. observed he had an amusing way of catching it. He simply gave it a light kick with the tip of his toe, almost like a skillful center forward can do with a soccer ball, and as a matter of fact the lamp bounced elegantly back up and obediently came to rest again at its place on the table.

It was clear that Belo would have been worth quite a few million as a left forward for a pro soccer team.

"As I was saying, what have the Utopians been concerned about all this time, from Plato to that unusually fat fellow from Trier, what was his name, Max or Maks or Mach? They've wanted to have a society where nothing would change anymore because everything was complete. Doesn't that fit in with what we have here? Have you seen anyone use a coin here or write out a check?"

"No, it strikes me I haven't."

"Absolutely correct. We have a moneyless society. We introduced it forty thousand years ago, when we discovered that all accounts ended the year with precisely the same balance they had at the beginning of the year, so it was an entirely unnecessary task to sit and run through every transaction annually."

"A moneyless society, fine. But it's also newspaperless."

"Well, that's not so odd. We have no war, no strikes, no fights or murders, no factory shutdowns to report. What do we need newspapers for, then? Philosophical discussions? But we have no philosophical problems. Philosophical problems exist only where people have something to be troubled about, but what do people need to be troubled about here?"

"That life is so very tedious."

"Believe me, dear friend—I don't at all want to be impertinent, but believe me—you're not at all typical of people in general. You're a typical, uneasy, European intellectual. You're not happy if you don't have anything to be troubled about. If you don't get to read at the breakfast table about some new military junta in Chile you can demonstrate against on Kurfürstendamm in the evening, you simply get indigestion. If you can't understand life as

164

a struggle with dark riddles, you can't find the right colors for your newest painting.

"That's all fine and dandy, but you have to realize you can't generalize about all people from yourself. What most people generally want is quiet. Peace and quiet. Four to five hours of work a day, getting up not too early in the morning, and a little beer and dart-throwing in the evening. No TV, no violent films, no mass bombing of poor countries to enjoy on the evening news, no gasoline price increases every other year. Just a little peace and quiet. We live a healthy life, you should be clear about that. Healthier on the whole than life can ever be in Berlin or the Federal Republic."

"I can say this much," said the painter G., and now with a great deal of conviction in her voice, "for my part, I'll never get on here. I'll go crazy, that's the plain truth."

Belo was silent. He had stopped swinging the tip of his foot up and down in that amusing way, and that was really a relief, for he had a very irritating way of doing it.

He looked at her attentively, without being either aggressive or friendly. It occurred to her that no one had ever looked at her that way before—it was the neutral gaze of a lizard or tortoise, its tongue flickering, inside the glass wall of a terrarium, looking out at the spectators, rather than the glance of an intelligent creature.

She perceived with a slight shudder that in this gentleman there had to be a weariness greater than in any other being she had ever met. The sympathy she had felt for him began to disappear. She suddenly saw that for Belo she was of no greater or less interest than a peculiarly colored stone on the road or a strangely shaped wooden stick.

His benevolent concern was nothing but an act, routine and skillful, of an old, shrewd diplomat who long ago learned how to make an impression on people and keep up as much contact with them as needed to get them where he wants.

That annoyed her all the more, because she understood completely that at bottom she was horribly fascinated by him.

165

She felt that if this conversation did not end soon, she would become angry, unpleasantly so, and there would be a scene—one of her big ones, she knew it.

"I'm sorry that this experiment has turned out so badly," said Belo. "So very badly."

And at that moment, of course, he really did look distressed.

"It's not so important politically or economically, even if we can't afford to lose too many opportunities of allying great talents with us. There's another matter that saddens me more, and that is that we won't have the opportunity to meet anymore. I've come to place great store in our interesting conversations."

"Sure thing, you old fraud," the painter G. thought. She had grown up in Moabit and at an early age already knew very well how old uncles can be. Now she was so furious that she decided to show no further traces of her anger.

Something, perhaps an imperceptible change in his attitude (he no longer seemed so fraternal) made G. understand that Belo considered the conversation as more or less finished. She began to be concerned about the trip home—would he make any effort whatsoever to bring her home sometime?—when he said:

"I gather you think you've seen enough. It's too bad, in a way. There are so many other interesting things here I really wanted to show you. Scenery that looks entirely different, really wild scenery. But I understand, it wouldn't be of much use. Lately, I've asked myself whether you aren't more of a portrait painter than a landscape artist."

"In a way," she answered.

"People interest you more than nature, isn't that right?"

"Yes."

"There's something that's interested me very much, which I'd really like to ask you about, if it doesn't seem too intrusive, now that our dealings are actually finished and, so it appears, wrecked. May I ask you about it?"

"Ask about what?"

166

"In Berlin, you said you'd like a very special clause in your contract."

"Yes."

"And that was to the effect that you could be another person for a single day and night. Isn't that right?"

"Yes."

"That is a very unusual request, you understand, much more unusual than you think."

"Really?"

"As a matter of fact, in my long experience I've never run into anyone who wanted something so strange. Not even torture victims writhing in ghastly pain, who want it to stop immediately, want something so strange."

"But I want it."

"Why, exactly?"

"Because I think it would give a key to all of history, almost to the whole of creation."

"How do you mean?"

(Belo now seemed quite seriously interested. It actually appeared that for once she had succeeded in arriving at a thought he had never entertained before.)

"But that's obvious. Your whole life you see the world through a single keyhole, from a single perspective, your own. Suppose you could change it! Naturally, you'd find that a few things you've always taken as obvious characteristics of reality are nothing more than some little idiosyncracy in your own brain, while that odd little anxiety you sometimes have, without being able to explain where it comes from, as a matter of fact is not at all some idiosyncracy of yours but a characteristic of reality itself—a sort of deep, muted, rumbling organ tone that all beings feel deep inside, the universe's own low tone of anxiety. From that day on, you'd feel free and you'd finally understand history, don't you see?"

Belo gazed at her thoughtfully for a long while. Deep within

167

his very weary, icy blue, reptilian eyes she caught a quick, lightning glimpse of something she never thought to find there—something that actually was not coldness, not unlimited weariness, something that both frightened her and made her happy.

What she saw in that brief, flashing moment was that somewhere, far back in a time before time, they were related to each other.

Belo hopped down from the edge of the table.

"You're a hell of a girl," he said abruptly.

The Flute Player in Kreuzberg

WHAT DO YOU WANT?
I WANT TO DIE AND YET LIVE
I WANT TO BE SOMEONE ELSE AND YET BE WHO I AM
I WANT TO BE LOVED BUT NOT BECAUSE OF MY
    MERITS
BUT BY CHANCE?
IT FRIGHTENS ME IF NO ONE LOVES ME
IT FRIGHTENS ME MORE IF SOMEONE LOVES ME
IF SELF-CONTRADICTIONS PREVENTED SOMETHING
    FROM EXISTING
I WOULD NEVER EXIST, PRECISELY:
HOW DO YOU KNOW YOU EXIST?
I THINK, THEREFORE I AM
ARE YOU CERTAIN THAT SOMEONE ELSE IS NOT
    THINKING IN YOUR STEAD?

You are absolutely right. I have considered the possibility of solving my problems by going crazy.

Ha! Easy you say! The first thing that will happen is that they will take me back to Sweden and lock me up in a place where they will pump so many pernicious chemicals into me, and run so many watts or kilowatts or megawatts through my poor, scarred brain, that I will simply no longer be able to keep myself on the intellectual level where a real mania could be played out with some artistry. I will quickly fall down through the protective net of tranquilizers to the level where they can offer me a nice job as a proofreader again. This society does not have the means to allow people to develop manias in peace. A properly played-out mania is something for wealthy, private people with respectable unmarried sisters who wash the dishes. If Nietzsche were living today, he would have had to apply for a scholarship.

So, forget it! Humanly and biologically, it is cheaper, practically speaking, to knock down a couple of policemen, and I suspect that the harm done to social prestige is less.

THE WALL TOWERS ALOFT, HIGH AND GRAY

The Berlin wall towers aloft, high and gray, far out into Kreuzberg. It rises, among shabby, decayed barracks, Gypsy camps, and automobile graveyards, with its high watchtowers, searchlights, and mined zones behind the ridge. And it is really not so remarkable.

Out here, where the plasterboard houses look like they have leprosy; where little Gypsy girls, dark and lively in their gaudy dresses play between wrecked cars and rubbish heaps; here, where the houses almost stand and lean toward the Wall, where there is a mysterious twinkle from the windows from dark, rattling textile factories—here everything seems completely natural.

It is, quite simply, the limit of the world.

Is that so incomprehensible? Why shouldn't the world have a limit?

Isn't it much more difficult to imagine a limitless, steadily expanding universe, where the galaxies are rushing apart from each other faster than shrapnel from a grenade blast?

I suspect that deep down I am against limits, as I have already said. But limits are practical.

At this particular limit, they shoot people now and then. You hear abrupt, sharp automatic weapons' fire in the nocturnal darkness. Someone screams. After a moment, you hear the ambulances on the other side.

Those who die pay the price for socialism, the price for East German currency's not sinking down to an untenable level.

Okay. You say that you are against people being shot to keep a currency on a reasonable level.

I am too. I am absolutely against people being shot at all. In Vietnam, they mass-bombed the population, and the dollar sank all the way to a dangerously low level.

I am against people being mass-bombed.

But that is what happens in the world, you see. Whether we are against it or not, it happens.

It is probably not so odd that you get a desire to flee into a really elegant, delicately balanced insanity.

If you think it is strange, that simply means you are privileged, dumb, without fantasies, and a little bit cruel.

I suspect that most of my readers are privileged, dumb, without fantasies, and a little bit cruel. Yet, I cannot point to exactly what I mean.

Too bad.

Right here, at this place out in Kreuzberg, the Wall has been brightened up noticeably. Someone has written on it, in red letters half a yard high:

MADE IN GERMANY

That is not so dumb. I know who wrote it.

One lovely afternoon at the end of May, when the chestnut trees are all in bloom and a fine, springlike drizzle is falling through the air, when I have come out to Kreuzberg to buy Turkish lamb—the Turks in Kreuzberg have such extremely good lamb—he suddenly stops in the street, huge and bearded, a regular satyr, and plays a flute for the traffic.

The drivers blow their horns wildly and swerve, their tires screeching. He does not let himself be bothered. The fragile sound of his flute goes right through the noise of the furious horns and perilously screeching tires. When the light turns red, he can be heard better. If I am not mistaken, he is playing a chaconne of the great François Couperin. The fine, chestnut-smelling rain becomes a bit heavier.

One of the few old German ladies in Kreuzberg, white-haired, with ramrod posture, a determined major's widow, crosses the street.

The flute player roguishly pinches her calf.

It had to be the first time in at least forty years that anyone had roguishly pinched her calf.

The expression on her face, when she shakes her umbrella at him with her fist, is indescribable.

How mysteriously Eros crosses the path of every procession from the side.

But the lady says someone really should call the police.

The flute player is Kreuzberg's sorcerer.

I call him that because once, at a party, someone seriously claimed that every section of Berlin has its own sorcerer.

Dahlem's sorcerer is an elegant old gentleman who looks like a professor and walks through subway cars politely distributing a pamphlet that deals with how the atoms in the universe are rapidly breaking up internally, which is leading to a catastrophe.

Moabit's sorcerer is a happy harlequin with bells in his cap who usually dances on the sidewalk outside the Schultheiss brewery on Turmstrasse.

With a fluttering black coat, on nights with a full moon, Lichterfelde's sorcerer throws himself down the hill where Otto Lilienthal tested his kites. But the sorcerer's kite does not fall. He sails away and disappears like a dot against the disc of the moon.

Kreuzberg's sorcerer does not fly. He plays his flute. Now he has moved onto a lawn in a park where he plays for a circle of children who stand around him and quickly split into two groups.

One group loves him, their eyes and mouths wide open. The other group hates him.

"*You dummy*," says a little Gypsy girl and looks at him with very black, hate-filled eyes.

And now, when the rain stops, birds are heard singing again.

On the street corners in Berlin, there are strange contraptions that look like outsized mailboxes with blue lamps on top. If you are assaulted by a robber, if there is a traffic accident, or God knows what, you are supposed to press the button. Then the blue lamp on top begins to rotate and flash, through a loudspeaker a metallic voice from the police station asks what you want. The idea is that you should say that someone is murdering you, or words to that effect, and a police car will find its way to the place, guided by the flashing blue light.

Now the flute player gets up and with springy satyr's steps walks over to one of those contraptions and cheerfully presses the button. The blue lamp begins to go around and flash, people stop and gather in a little circle around him.

As I have mentioned, there are birds singing. Thrushes, blackbirds, an occasional lark are heard from a vacant lot close by.

And now the flute player begins to imitate the birdsongs. A perfect illusion, loud and strong, he pipes all the trills of the larks, the thrushes, and the blackbirds into that stupid contraption.

It is an extremely unbelievable wind concert.

He gives the same concert all over again, even more brilliant more joyful, and with even more intricate trills and cadenzas than before. Then he takes his flute, plays a little cheerful melody, and whispers ironically and happily into the contraption, which just seems to sit there hiccupping from surprise:

KEINE LEICHE IN DIESER ECKE—no dead body on this
    corner
KEINE LEICHE IN DIESER ECKE

It is a very funny moment, and everyone standing around applauds.

Just at that moment, I realize I have been looking at a young man standing opposite me in the circle and that we have greeted each other absentmindedly.

Only when the young man, thin, dark-haired, with big, wise, somewhat ironic eyes, has disappeared into the crowd again, does

173

something occur to me that makes me want a firmer grip on my senses, and I massage my temples hard with my knuckles.

The person I saw a second ago is entirely unfamiliar. I have never known this young man.

But I can swear I greeted him because I recognized him, because I really do know him well.

The young man in the elegant leather jacket and the big, wise eyes was none other than the painter G.!

None other than the painter G.

Or could I just be mistaken?

KEINE LEICHE IN DIESER ECKE

II

Sigismund Walks Again

The Matter and Yet Not the Matter

Endless are the potato fields of Purgatory, like a muddy Prussia in November where a mild rain is pattering down.

Corner houses between Kantstrasse and Fasanenstrasse, more or less a red-light district, with neon signs and an occasional stray Yugoslav or Turk standing and pissing in a doorway in the evening. He has gotten too far away from the railway station, from Bahnhof am Zoo, which otherwise is the secure maternal embrace, the gateway to the homeland, the gathering place and clubroom where his pals are.

And the other evening I saw two figures staggering along on the sidewalk who seemed so strangely familiar, one a little taller than the other, and not until we met under the streetlight did I recognize them with a start. Good God! It was those drunk Finnish seamen, I mean those two drunk Finnish seamen who tried to get through the gate at Hagagatan one winter night in 1970 and whom an anxious woman talked me into throwing out again. *Good God, how did they end up here?*

One of them was mysteriously waving a paper at me just as we met. For a moment, it struck me that it could be a message for me, but since he did not seem especially persistent, I walked on.

A message for me, what a ridiculous idea. From whom would it be coming? They had to have been on the road for a long time.

IF THERE IS A RING AT THE DOOR, I DON'T THINK I'LL OPEN

Or: the matter and yet not the matter, as Goethe says when he talks about symbols.

The kitchen. It is a damn nuisance when I have to clean up. The wife and kids went back to Sweden two weeks ago. Plates with dried egg, grease, the coffee cup a French critic put out a cigarette in three days ago, all the slovenly tristesse of solitary eating.

(A person who eats is not unappetizing, but a person who eats alone is.)

Breadcrumbs on the floor, bundles of *Dagens Nyheter* in the corner, and here is an old *Scientific American*, the September issue, butter smeared between the pages

GOOD GOD, WHO SMEARS BUTTER IN MY MAGAZINES

with a big popular-science article on asymmetries in arithmetic, and the floor full of breadcrumbs that crunch under the feet and are tough and leave traces behind which press into the carpet. And just as I am holding the mop under the faucet, there is a gurgle and no more water. Turned off in the whole building! Not a drop!

The matter and yet not the matter, as the ingenious Goethe says, and Professor Kennedy across the hall, who usually loans me his vacuum cleaner, of course, had gone to Tokyo to lecture on city planning and would not return before some time next week.

I cannot describe it better, but that is the way it gets to look. You damn well better not forget it is written by a substitute. The real me could have written it much better.

But he is hiding in a sarcophagus in Cracow, the old black-guard! What the hell am I supposed to do except write in his place!

And everything a cursed boulder that has to be rolled up a hill. You grab hold, the veins in your forehead grow to the size of pencils, your ears turn blue, you get the bastard moving again, and then you roll it a little more, until it stops on the next plateau.

And it is so late in November that the light is already dim in the kitchen, or is it me who is beginning to get old and dim sighted?

Why doesn't he come? Sigismund, if I had you here, I would sock you in the mouth, you slugabed, you dullard, you sleepy dolt!

Like Job, yes just like Job. Like Job on his mound, on his bundle of newspapers that all tell about what we knew would happen, with a dry miserable mop in my hand and breadcrumbs that crunch under my feet. And potato fields! Right out to the horizon, those damned Prussian potato fields with their autumnal smell of rotting roots and tops that have been piled up burned in small heaps, so warm firelight dots the plain, and the avenues of willows that strut on toward the horizon.

HOW LONG WILL I YET REMAIN IN THESE ENDLESS POTATO FIELDS?

Then the water pipe begins to bubble and behave. It reverberates in the drained faucet, reverberates and bubbles, and with the last bubbling the water comes back again, spurting out of the wide-open faucet and soaking half the kitchen.

It spurts over my glasses, so that the world is seen as through an aquarium. The floor mop quickly becomes sopping, and two yards of old *Dagens Nyheter* too. Spray on my forehead, and now the sound of water is heard everywhere.

That is the sign. We begin again. We never give up.

And down on the street this bright morning, two drunks stagger from one side of the sidewalk to the other.

Where have I seen them before?

I lean dangerously far out of the window to see whether they are going to try to get in through my gate here at Kantstrasse, too. But suddenly they are gone, as if swallowed up by the earth.

And a gust of wind slams the window shut, hard. Another kind of wind, a strange wind that I had almost forgotten.

IF THERE IS A RING AT THE DOOR, I DON'T THINK I'LL OPEN

At the next moment, of course, the doorbell rings.

Mirror Worlds

Sergeant Reinhardt Klotz, of the East German Peoples' Police, a small, good-natured man with bloodshot eyes, thin reddish-blond hair, and ears that are too large, was just scratching himself behind the right one.

An unusual phenomenon for the month of November, a tremendous thunderstorm with heavy hail, was sweeping over the two halves of the city. The policemen who had the job of inspecting the passing vehicles at Checkpoint Charlie were already soaking wet, their raincoats pattering under the already pea-sized hail.

An eccentric man in an old American Buick, registered in Panama, could in such circumstances smuggle in no less than twelve copies of Pseudo-Dionysius the Areopagite's *On the Celestial Hierarchy*, elegantly concealed in the car's hubcaps.

The hail made it completely impossible to stand and root around in the cars' interiors for long.

In the narrow corridor of the waiting room at the checkpoint, there was a sharp smell of beeswax and disinfectant. Two not entirely sober Finnish seamen came up time after time to the window with their currency declarations more or less bizarrely filled out, were made to do them over again by Corporal Alexander Kluge, and crestfallen they rambled back to the little writing table. They had already used up a substantial number of forms, and their Finnish conversation became a little louder each time.

Sergeant Klotz, grandson of the popular potato merchant and amateur painter Walter Klotz of Magdeburg, who himself grew up in Bitterfeld as the sixth son of the bricklayer Henzel Klotz and his wife Edeltraut Klotz, often had trouble looking like a cop. He frequently had difficulty fixing his eyes on the travelers in the correct, prescribed manner. When he stared that way, he had a feeling the travelers were gazing at his ears instead.

That often made him uncertain.

Sergeant Klotz fixed his eyes for the fourth time on the young man in the black leather jacket and dark blue corduroy jeans who was standing in front of him, seeking entry to his homeland.

The young man had a rather sharply defined profile, short dark hair, a discreet, equally dark mustache, and very large, intelligent eyes. He did not look like an imperialist agent. The instruction manual nevertheless warned against drawing hasty conclusions from a person's appearance.

The young man looked well bred and rather attractive. It really was not he who was causing Sergeant Klotz trouble but the strange passport with violet covers he had handed over for inspection.

Sergeant Klotz was an experienced man. Gaudy bundles of Saudi-Arabian, Australian, British, Monacan, Danish, and Finnish passports passed through his hands daily. Once a month or so, a passport from the Kingdom of Bhutan or the Republic of Chad showed up. There was not anything strange about that. They were examined, the photograph, hair color, eye color, and the shape of the ears were compared with the travelers. The passports were carried in bundles to a senior official, who checked if they were forged and whether the person in question was on the list of undesirables. And after a shorter or longer wait, they could be returned to the counter again.

There was actually nothing remarkable about it. But this passport the devil himself could not figure out. The inside was embellished with an unusually stylish coat of arms that depicted a knight in armor holding an inverted torch in his right hand. An archaic script, probably Gothic in origin, in which a serif trailed backward like a flame from every ascender, clearly indicated that the holder of this passport was a citizen of Thinth, and that the authorities of Thinth were asking all authorities with whom the person in question came in contact to help him and facilitate his trip to the best of their ability.

Klotz disappeared for the fourth time into the office of Sergeant Major Reichenbach, who was already going through the regulations frantically.

181

"Thinth, is that a kingdom or republic?" shouted Reichenbach. "It's not on the passport."

At this moment, Klotz caught sight of a surprisingly large black crow that had obviously settled down for good on the sergeant major's narrow desk.

"How in God's name did it get in here?" roared the sergeant major. "Get it out!"

"It must be the hail. It was naturally looking for protection here," said Klotz, who in his freetime was an enthusiastic member of the Ornithological Society of Köpenick and an ardent bird watcher.

"Maybe we could open the window," said Klotz carefully, conscious of the bad humor of his immediate superior.

"Sergeant, are you out of your mind! Open the window? In this weather, every paper will blow away! Damn it, pick the animal up and take it away!"

Klotz made a serious attempt to approach the crow in as ornithologically correct a manner as possible. It flapped its wings and settled high up on a brown-painted file cabinet. Outside in the waiting room corridor was heard a cautiously rising murmur. Not a single traveler had been taken care of for quite a while, and people were crowding the abandoned counters. The drunken Finnish seamen had given up their useless struggle with the forms and were sleeping securely, propped up against each other on a bench. It looked like nothing could bother them anymore.

"Good God, there's another one here," said the sergeant major, jumping up from his desk. It was flapping madly around his feet. The sergeant major began nervously to finger his holster. But fortunately realizing it would be a serious breach of regulations to start shooting at crows inside the guardhouse, with a swift kick he succeeded in freeing himself from the beast, which fluttered up to the ceiling. And then the two crows began a most bizarre round dance up there, so that the ceiling light swayed and papers flew off the desk.

A fresh, strong hailstorm swept over the checkpoint. The

182

crows suddenly flapped out the door right across the waiting room with a strangely conscious flight, and disappeared into the rainy November day.

"Damn strange," said Reichenbach, "mighty damn strange what such weather can bring on."

"Thinth, was it," said Klotz. With an irritated grunt, Reichenbach handed back the passport from Thinth. *"Is it really necessary to bother me all the time with trifles?* Everyone knows where Thinth is. Now try to do a little work!"

"Thanks very much," said the young man in a pleasant baritone voice, and put the passport in his pocket.

A few minutes later, he was crossing Alexanderplatz with quick steps. It was blowing so hard, the sausage vendor down by the World Clock at one corner of the huge square seriously began to worry about how his stand would stay up if the wind increased further in strength. The young man in the leather jacket continued calmly, all but whistling it seemed, down toward the huge new high-rises at Fischerinsel.

But inside the leather jacket . . . inside the leather jacket, there was a supple, well-trained body trying in vain to understand itself.

NOT A SINGLE THING WAS FAMILIAR

In the first hours, the painter G. had the sensation you get when you step into an elevator and unexpectedly discover that all the signs are written in Arabic or Japanese.

She had already discovered that she probably had had chronic rheumatism in her left knee for the past eight years, because she suddenly realized that a well-functioning left knee feels entirely different than hers used to. She also found out that she had been nearsighted for the past few years, since there was not a single sign she could not read with these excellent, new brown eyes.

But these were small matters, amusing trifles compared to everything else she discovered.

The fact was THE COLORS WERE NOT REALLY THE SAME. Blue looked like "blue," "red" like red, that's true, but it was not the same red, not the same blue. The new blue had a more metallic nuance that it used to have for her, the new red a microscopic hint of higher color temperature.

She was bothered quite a lot by this strange thing which for the moment was located in the left leg of her corduroy pants.

It had an odd tendency to live its own life. And it radiated a constant, not at all unpleasant anxiety. It seemed to want something all the time, always talking to her.

She had never imagined it would feel *that* way.

What bothered her most and made her get a grip on herself time after time, so as not to fall into panic, was another thing, the strange fear of *the unknown*. It was the same fear you sometimes feel when it is very crowded in the subway and it suddenly becomes completely quiet as the train stops somewhere far down the line, the same noticeable fear mixed with pleasure you feel when you have become acquainted with an exciting girl late in the evening in some little bar and disappear with her in a taxi *far into the night*, while the rain washes over the streets and makes the asphalt shine.

This fear mixed with pleasure (only much stronger, much more intense) was felt all the while by the painter G., or the person who had recently been the painter G. and who was now someone else.

But who was she really? And what does it mean to be a human being?

(A Hebrew poet, one of my best friends, had to go to war against the Egyptians in the fall of 1973. He saw the great tank battles, the white flashes from the heavy, long-range artillery, he saw the black lumps of charred men sitting at the wheels of burned trucks. He came back and wrote a poem that in Hebrew contains only five words:

184

"—What is that?

—It was a man.")

There is fear, and there is fear. If a car comes toward you at high speed on the wrong side of the road, that is one kind of fear. If your wife tells you she is leaving you, that is another kind, and it is very different from the first. There is also the fear called "horror."

Horror is the ancient fear of something not alive, or that should not be alive, turning out to be alive after all. Horror is what we feel about ghosts.

Horror is the kind of fear we feel when we imagine our own life could be simulated.

This was the horror she felt now: who am I? And blended with the horror was the wildest pleasure: *far into the night*.

The high-rises on Fischerinsel have the most troublesome elevators in all of East Berlin. She had not been there in years and, for her, all of the buildings were completely new. They must have been built sometime during the fall or winter of 1970–71.

It took her a long while to discover that in these new buildings, you had to press on a special button to close the door before the automatic elevator would move. It is a sensible arrangement in a building with lots of children.

Margret was a childhood friend. She remembered her from high school dances as a very pale girl, always in dresses a little too short, with unusually big, blue eyes. Now she was living here.

They had stayed in touch over the years. Margret had got married in East Berlin and then had managed to get divorced.

Now she stood at the door of her apartment and looked with surprise at the young man in the leather jacket. Suddenly, she smiled.

"You're the brother of G., the painter, aren't you," she said. "Come in!"

She had not changed very much over the years. She was still very pretty. All at once, the painter G. felt very calm.

She understood what it was she had wanted all the while.

She hung her leather jacket on a chair and sat down. Under her black tee-shirt, you could see the strong muscles of her shoulders.

She was, without a doubt, a very handsome man.

"Can I offer you some vodka," her old childhood friend said, and for a moment held her very white, well-preserved hand on the back of the chair behind G.

It was a rather smart, extremely well-kept apartment. A transistor radio sat on a glass shelf. The walls were lined with books. The radio was reporting about the bicycle industry's splendid increases in productivity. Honecker had opened the new writers' conference. The clock read a quarter after four.

The soft winter light was passing over into early winter evening. The lights in the buildings around Alexanderplatz were lit, one by one.

And look, now the first, doubtful snowflakes were beginning to fall over the German Democratic Republic in the winter of 1973.

"This is what I wanted. This is what I've wanted the whole time," the painter G. said to herself:

A MIRROR WORLD

A MIRROR WORLD TO UNDERSTAND WHAT MAN-KIND IS

"I'd love a drink," she said.

Ever warmer, ever more friendly to her seemed the light behind the curtains that her childhood friend now was closing, one by one.

The King's Return

NO, I WON'T OPEN IF THERE IS A RING AT THE DOOR

I said to myself and continued to remove old dried egg from the plates that had not been washed for three days in my kitchen on Kantstrasse. I do not want to have anything more to do with those seamen. It would be bourgeois sentimentality to think that the world will improve if they get a couple of coins for beer. They will just get drunk again.

Now the door rang for the third time. And since I did not care to open it, something began to rattle violently at the mailbox.

I went out into the hall with the dishcloth, ready to strike. "There's such a thing as law and order," I thought.

The mailbox lid had in fact been opened from the outside. Two blue eyes were staring unremittingly at me in the hall. The narrow mailbox slot with the staring blue eyes was so ridiculously like the trademark on the wrapping of Marabou's Eye Chocolate that I could not help laughing.

"Open up," said the voice behind the mailbox slit, in a strong, Finnish singsong, "open up, damn it!"

"No," I said.

"You shall open up for the King."

"What damn King?"

"The King."

"Don't try any tricks," I said.

"I come from Savolaks, and I don't try tricks," said the voice on the other side. A terrific smell of booze came through the mailbox slit.

"No," I said.

The mailbox lid shut with a bang. I heard some annoyed replies in Finnish behind the door, and then they disappeared down the steps.

I returned to my dishes and found that the water had run over onto the counter because some leftover potatoes had effectively blocked the drain. There was at least a quarter of an inch of water covering the whole kitchen floor.

"Remarkable," I said to myself, "either there's too little water or too much, either as dry as a bone or a flood—there's no order in this building anymore, that's the plain truth."

Annoyed, I returned to my desk and tried to do a little work. I had hardly gotten a few lines into it when a horrible commotion out on Kantstrasse disturbed me so much that I went over to the window to see what in God's name was going on. Judging from the wild honking coming from below, it would seem the entire street was blocked.

I opened the window. The noise was really earsplitting. A line of cars seemed to stretch from my street corner practically all the way to Savignyplatz.

Some drivers had even got out of their cars and were standing on the street shaking their fists.

The police alarm on the corner of Kantstrasse and Fasanenstrasse was wildly spinning its blue light, and a little figure was dancing, crazy with joy, around the contraption. I leaned as far out as I dared, and it was the sorcerer of Kreuzberg indeed, dancing happily, in turn playing his flute and singing, in a high and scornful voice:

KEINE LEICHE AN DIESER ECKE, KEINE LEICHE AN DIESER ECKE

At first, I thought that was the cause of the traffic jam (the line of wildly honking cars and the series of clenched fists and swearing drivers now stretched it seemed all the way up to Ernst-Reutherplatz).

With a final, perilous lean out the window, I discovered that the cause was outside my own gate.

An immense, shiny black Oldsmobile, with a horn outside and

a leather-clad chauffeur, had quite simply stopped in the middle of the block in front of my gate.

Four motorcycle police in white leather outfits surrounded the magnificent vehicle on all sides and were now leaning nonchalantly against their machines, their gloves on their seats and their cigarettes in holders, completely uninterested in the hellish noise behind them.

A pennant fluttered on each of the Oldsmobile's shiny black, well-polished front fenders.

A gust of wind started the pennants moving—it was on the whole a day with a great deal of movement in the air—and with a twinge of discomfort I saw that it was as I had suspected all along: the car bore the medieval Polish coat of arms, with its characteristic eagles.

I decided to pretend I had nothing to do with the matter.

One minute later, there was another ring on the door. I realized that if I did not open, I could not help but make a painful situation even more painful.

The first thing I saw were the Finnish seamen, but now clad in black velvet suits with lace frills on the neckbands and sleeves, patent-leather shoes, and charming reddish-purple sashes of moiré silk around their waists. Not unlike young princes, they swung their ceremonial staffs of ebony with knobs of chased silver. There was a very strong smell around them of peppermint drops and Eau Sauvage, and some skillful barber had done wonders with their hair.

Without a word, they came to attention at either side of the door.

The gentleman who now stepped out through the elevator door, clad in an elegant suit of the best English tweed, was short rather than tall.

He did not seem a day over sixty and moved with indescribable dignity.

Everything—the square white beard, the rather prominent

cheekbones, the ample nose—fit perfectly with the six portraits that are kept at Gripsholm castle.

I made an ironically deep bow.

Without vouchsafing me a glance, he marched into my living room, positioning himself to view the scene outside the window. A steam locomotive followed by many freight cars passed over the railroad bridge above Kantstrasse. The drivers were still honking their horns like madmen out there. He glanced at the clock on the Gedächtnis Church tower and pedantically compared it to his own diamond-studded pocket watch that he hauled up from his vest. He shook his head. Apparently, the times did not agree at all.

Slowly he turned away from the window and sized me up at a glance. His eyes were magnificent, clear blue, bright. They were the eyes of a wise man. Without further ceremony, he began to speak:

"Blackguard! Numbskull! Clod! Liar! It's about time I caught up with you, you dunderhead!

"Outer space—bah!" He made an indescribable grimace, displaying in this way something of the Vasa family's rustic candor. "And what in hell do you think you're doing, putting me in a picture on an outhouse in Ramnäs? You think I'm some kind outhouse character?

"Young man, it's about time to pull yourself together! The serpent of time changes skin, young man, do you understand that?

"The lock at Färmansbo—that's right, you had it there, young man, but you lost it again! The flowing water that's important! Everything is flowing water, black eddies, cascades, white foam through old lock gates—on it must flow.

"Do you know your pre-Socratics? They say that everything flows, everything is water streaming away, everything is an old lock with large alders above the water and black eddies where the pike hide. You have to understand, too: it isn't for nothing that water flows.

"Bah—"

He stuck out his tongue in an indescribable rustic grimace. It was medieval and at the same time royal, just as primitively expressive as the gargoyles in the shape of mythological beasts on Gothic cathedrals sticking out their tongues.

"Your Majesty," I answered, "your Majesty, in your absence I have done my best."

A Note on the Author

Lars Gustafsson was born on May 17, 1936, in Västerås, Sweden. He earned the equivalent of an American doctorate at the University of Uppsala in 1962, and his dissertation, *Language and Lies*, on Friedrich Nietzsche, Fritz Mauthner, and the American philosopher Alexander Bryan Johnson (under whom the author studied), has been published in several languages.

Through his writings on mathematics, sociology, history, philosophy, and literature, Gustafsson's influence has been strong in all quarters of the European academic community, but his essays and comments, notably the collection on *Utopia* (1969), have reached an even broader audience. He has published in virtually every area of *belles lettres*: novels, stories, poems, drama, literary criticism, and journalism, and from 1962 to 1972, he was the editor of *Bonniers Litterära Magasin*, the leading literary periodical of Sweden.

He is best known in his native land and, through an excellent translation, in Germany as well, for his related series of novels, *Mr. Gustafsson, Himself* (1971), *Woe* (1973), *Family Reunion* (1975), *Sigismund* (1977), and *The Death of a Beekeeper* (1979). Although each of these can be enjoyed alone, they are five variations on a common theme: "We begin again. We never give up."